Too Many Clues for Comfort

"The murderer knew Ralph's meticulous nature. He would have counted on Ralph's using the flasks from the left-hand side and of running precisely one experiment each day. That would make the poisoned one come up on a Thursday when Ralph would be alone in the laboratory . . . the murderer was right at home with the necessary conditions."

"What are you getting at, Lou?"

"Just that the police will list all these requirements, too, and find the one person that best fits them."

"Who?"

"Myself, my dear. I am the one likely suspect that fits all the facts. *The only possible suspect.*"

Fawcett Crest Mysteries
by Isaac Asimov:

ASIMOV'S MYSTERIES   23223-9 $1.50

MURDER AT THE ABA   23202-6 $1.75

TALES OF THE BLACK WIDOWERS   22944-0 $1.50

MORE TALES OF THE BLACK WIDOWERS
  23375-8 $1.50

THE CAVES OF STEEL   23782-6 $1.75

THE NAKED SUN   22648-4 $1.50

ISAAC ASIMOV

A Whiff of Death

FAWCETT CREST • NEW YORK

A WHIFF OF DEATH

THIS BOOK CONTAINS THE COMPLETE TEXT OF
THE ORIGINAL HARDCOVER EDITION.

Published by Fawcett Crest Books, a unit of CBS Publications,
the Consumer Publishing Division of CBS Inc., by
arrangement with Walker and Company.

ISBN: 0-449-23660-9

Originally published under the title *The Death Dealers*

Printed in the United States of America

10 9 8 7 6 5 4 3 2 1

A Whiff of Death

1

DEATH sits in the chemistry laboratory and a million people sit with him and don't mind.

They forget he's there.

Louis Brade, Assistant Professor of Chemistry, would, however, never forget that little fact again. He slumped in the chair in the cluttered student laboratory, sitting with Death, and very conscious of it. More conscious of it, in fact, now that the police were gone and the corridors were empty once more. More conscious of it now that the lab had been cleared of the physical evidence of mortality in the shape of Ralph Neufeld's body.

But Death was still there. He hadn't been touched.

Brade removed his glasses and polished them slowly with a clean handkerchief that he kept for that one use, then paused to look at the double reflection, one in each lens, each broadened in the middle by the trick of glass-curvature so that his spare face looked full and his wide, thin-lipped mouth wider.

No deeper marks, he wondered. Hair as dark as it was three hours ago, face lined about the eyes (as was fitting at forty-two), but no more lined than before all this?

Surely, one couldn't deal with Death so closely and not be marked in some way.

He replaced his glasses and looked about the laboratory again. Why be marked by meeting Death a little more closely this once? He met him, after all, every day, every moment, in every direction.

Look at him there, sitting in half a hundred reagent bottles of brown glass, crowding the shelves. Each bottle of Death was clearly labelled, each filled in varying amounts with its particular kind of fine, pure crystals. Most of them looked like salt.

Salt could kill, of course. Take enough of it and it will kill. But most of the crystals in those bottles would do the job much more quickly than salt would. Some would manage it in a minute or less in the proper dosage.

Quickly, slowly, painfully or not; each one was a sovereign cure for earthly misery and from their use no relapse into life was possible.

Brade sighed. To the oblivious ones who used them, they might as well be salt. They were funneled onto sheets of weighing paper or into flasks, dissolved in water, spilt or splashed on work-bench tops and brushed idly away or wiped up with a paper towel.

All those drops and crumbs of Death were moved to one side to make room, perhaps, for a sandwich. Or a beaker that had but lately held the Great Leveller might be used again for orange juice.

The shelves held lead acetate, called sugar of lead because it tasted sweet as it killed you. There was barium nitrate, copper sulfate, sodium dichromate, dozens of others, death-dealers all.

And potassium cyanide, of course. Brade had thought the police would impound it, but they only viewed it from a distance and left it there with its better than half a pound of Death inside.

In the cabinets below the laboratory bench were the five-liter bottles of strong acids, including sulfuric acid that could blind in a careless spurt and leave you with a scar for a face. In one corner were compressed gas cylinders, some a foot long, and some almost as tall as a man. Any one of them could explode desperately if a few simple precautions were neglected or, in some cases, poison insidiously.

Death by force or by stealth, by mouth or by nose; or even bit by bit over the years, as with the mercury droplets that would surely glitter across floor cracks and hidden corners in evil brightness if the dust that covered them were removed.

In every way, Death was there and no one minded. And then, once in a while, as now, one of those who sat with him did not rise again, ever.

Brade had walked into the student laboratory three hours earlier. His oxygenation reaction was proceeding busily and his fresh new oxygen cylinder, which had just been maneuvered into place, was bleeding oxygen gas slowly into the reaction system. It was set for the night; he had one last little task and then he would return home for his five o'clock appointment with old Cap Anson.

As he explained afterward, it was his custom to nod good-evening to those of his students who were in their labs at the time he left for the day. And, in addition, it had been his intention to borrow a small quantity of standardized tenth-molar hydrochloric acid and Ralph Neufeld, as everyone knew, had the most meticulously standardized reagents in the building.

He found Ralph Neufeld slumped across the soapstone surface inside the hood with his face turned away from the door.

Brade frowned. For an intense student like Neufeld that was a most unorthodox pose. The proper young chemist, when conducting an experiment within a hood, kept the movable window of safety glass lowered between himself and the simmering chemicals. He kept the inflammable, noxious fumes safely within the enclosed area of the hood to be carried up by the fan to the exhaust on the roof.

One would not expect to see the window up and the experimenter resting his head on one elbow inside.

Brade said, "Ralph!" and stepped over to the student casually, footsteps light on the cork composition floor (intended to bounce dropped glassware unbroken) and at the touch of his hand Neufeld's body moved stiffly. With sudden, startled energy, Brade turned the student's head so that the face came into view. The blond, close-cut hair fell in tight waves as usual. Neufeld's eyes greeted him with a glassy stare from under half-open lids.

What is there that so sharply distinguishes the face of one dead from that of one sleeping or drunk?

It *was* death. Brade's hand found Ralph Neufeld pulseless and perceptibly cooled and his chemist's nose caught the faint traces and lingering remains of an almond odor.

Brade swallowed dryly and called the Medical School three blocks down, managing to keep his voice at almost its ordinary timber. He asked for Dr. Shulter, who he knew, and got him. Then he called the police.

He next called the department head, but Professor Arthur Littleby, it turned out, was gone and had been gone since lunch. He told Littleby's secretary, for the record, what he had found and what he had done and warned her to avoid spreading the news for a time.

Then he crossed over to his own lab and closed off the oxygen, opening his reaction system and removing the heated jacket. Let it come to a halt. It had no importance at the moment. He stared at the gauges of the tall oxygen cylinder, unseeingly trying to absorb the facts and not entirely succeeding.

Then, feeling himself in the middle of a great and empty silence, he turned back to the dead student's laboratory, made sure its door was closed and on the latch, and sat down with Death to wait.

Dr. Ivan Shulter of the Medical School knocked gently on the door and Brade let him in. Shulter's examination was not prolonged. He said, "He's been dead for a couple of hours. Cyanide!"

Brade nodded. "I had supposed that."

Shulter brushed gray hair back off his forehead and exposed more of a sleek face that obviously perspired easily and was glistening now. He said, "Well, this will make a stink. It would be this one, of course."

Brade said, "Do you—did you know him?"

"I've met him. He takes books out of the medical library and then won't return them. I had to send a gaggle of librarians out after him to get a volume I needed and he reduced one of them to tears by being quite nasty about it. But it doesn't matter now, I suppose."

He left.

The medical man brought in by the police agreed with the diagnosis, made a few brisk notations and disappeared. Pictures were taken from three angles and then what was left of Neufeld was wrapped in a sheet and carried out.

A chunky plainclothesman remained behind. He introduced himself, with a flash of card, as Jack Doheny. His cheeks sagged plumply, and his voice had a bass rasp to it.

He said, "Ralph Neufeld," spelling it out painstakingly, then showing it to Brade for confirmation. "Any close relatives we can get in touch with?"

Brade looked up thoughtfully. "He has a mother. The office will have her address."

"We'll check. Now how'd it happen, Prof? Just for the record."

"I don't know. I found him this way."

"Was he having troubles with his studies?"

"No, he was doing well. Are you thinking of suicide?"

"They use cyanide for that sometimes."

"But why should he set up an experiment if all he wanted was suicide?"

Doheny looked about the lab dubiously. "You tell me, Prof. Could it have been an accident? This ain't exactly my line." He waggled a blunt thumb at the chemicals.

Brade said, "It might have been an accident, yes. It might have been. Ralph was running a number of experiments in which he had to dissolve sodium acetate in the reaction mixture. . . ."

"Hold it. Sodium what kind of acid?"

Brade spelled it patiently and Doheny wrote it down just as patiently. Brade went on, "The mixture is kept boiling and then, at a certain time after the acetate addition, the mixture is acidified so that acetic acid is formed."

"Is acetic acid poisonous?"

"Not particularly. It's in vinegar. In fact, it's what gives vinegar its odor. Acetic acid has a strong vinegar smell. The point is, though, that Ralph must have used sodium cyanide to begin with instead of sodium acetate."

"How come? Do they look alike?"

"See for yourself." Brade reached for the reagent bottles of sodium cyanide and sodium acetate on the shelves. Both were of brown glass some six inches tall and both had labels of identical design. The sodium cyanide bottle carried the red word POISON.

Brade unscrewed the plastic top of each bottle and Doheny peered inside gingerly.

He said, "Mean to say these things always stay that close together on the shelf?"

Brade said, "The bottles are arranged alphabetically."

"Don't you keep the cyanide locked up?"

"No." Brade was beginning to feel the strain of having to watch each statement he made in order to avoid the irreparable false step.

Doheny frowned. "Hey, you're in trouble, Prof. If this kid's relatives want to make a fuss about negligence, the university's liable to find its lawyers getting a work-out."

Brade shook his head. "Not at all. Half the reagents— uh, chemicals, you see on the shelves are quite poisonous. Chemists know about that and are careful. You know your own gun is loaded, don't you? You don't shoot yourself with it."

"That's all right for chemists, maybe, but this was just a student, right?"

"Not *just* a student. Ralph got his bachelor's degree— graduated college, that is—four years ago. He's been doing graduate work toward his master's and doctor's ever since. He was fully qualified to work without supervision and he did. All our Ph.D. candidates do. In fact, they help supervise the undergraduate laboratories."

"Did he work here all alone?"

"No, not really. We keep the candidates two to a lab. Ralph's current roommate was Gregory Simpson."

"Was he in today?"

"No. Thursday's Simpson's big day for classes. He doesn't come in at all on Thursdays. Not in this lab anyway."

"So this kid, Ralph Neufeld, was all alone."

"That's right."

Doheny said, "Was this Neufeld a good student?"

"Excellent."

"How come he made the mistake then? I mean, if he used the cyanide, he would miss the vinegar smell and he'd get out of there fast, wouldn't he?"

The plainclothesman's face was as round and as harmless as it had been a moment before, his expression was as artless, but Brade frowned.

He said, "The absence of the vinegar smell might have been the point that proved fatal. When sodium cyanide is acidified, hydrogen cyanide is formed. This is a gas at boiling-water temperatures and would come fuming out with the steam. It is extremely poisonous."

Doheny said, "It's what they use in the gas-chambers out in the West?"

"That's right. They acidify a cyanide and form the gas. Now Ralph was working in a hood with a fan built in that would carry off most of the fumes, but even so he could have caught the vinegar smell if it had been there. But this time he didn't and he would have thought something was wrong, just as you said."

"Uh huh."

"But instead of running, his first reaction was probably to lean closer and sniff harder. No chemist should smell vapors unless he knows what it is he is smelling or unless he takes extreme precautions to smell very little of it, but still, in a moment of surprise, I can see Ralph forgetting himself."

"You mean, looking for the vinegar, he leaned over and dragged in a man-sized lungful."

"I think so. He had his head far into the hood when I found him."

"And went out like a light."

"Just about."

"Uh huh. Say, Prof, is it all right if I smoke, or will the place go up like a powderhouse?"

"It's safe at the moment."

Doheny lit a cigar with an expression of too-long-deferred contentment and said, "Let's get it straight now, Prof. Here's a kid who wants to use sodium ac-e-tate (hey, I'm getting to say it like a professional) only he doesn't. He reaches over here and gets the wrong bottle off the shelf, like this."

Doheny lifted the cyanide bottle from its place on the shelf and held it gingerly. "He carries it over here and adds some. What does he do? Sprinkle it out."

"He'd lift some out with a spatula, a small flat metal blade, and weigh it in a little container."

"All right. He does something." He moved the reagent bottle about and put it on the desk near the hood. He stared at the bottle and then at Brade. "And that's it?"

"I suppose that's it," said Brade.

"That fits in with what you found when you walked into the lab. You didn't find anything funny about the situation? Anything at all?"

It seemed to Brade that the detective's eyes were glinting shrewdly (tension was making him imaginative, he decided) but he shook his head and said, "No. Do you?"

Doheny shrugged. He scratched at his thinning hair with a forefinger and said, "Accidents kinda happen anywhere and especially in a place where you keep asking for it like here." He closed the small notebook in which he had been writing and put it in his inner jacket pocket.

He said, "We can always reach you here, can't we, Professor, in case there's some points gotta be cleared up?"

"Of course."

"That's it, then. And if you want some advice from outside, Prof, from a layman, like you say, keep the cyanide locked up."

"I'll consider it," said Brade, diplomatically. "Oh, and by the way, Ralph had a key to this laboratory. Could it be returned here if there's nothing you need it for?"

"Sure. Well, take care of yourself, Professor. Watch out for those labels on the bottles. Don't you mix them up!"

"I'll try not to," said Brade.

And now Brade could stand alone in the laboratory once more, stare at his own face in the lenses of his glasses and look at Death's face everywhere else in the room.

He thought of his wife. Doris would undoubtedly be worried. She expected him home early since Cap Anson was coming over at 5 P.M. (Good Lord! the punctual Cap was going to be hurt and censorious, Brade thought uneasily. He would certainly take this as a personal insult to his precious manuscript. And yet—how could it have been helped?)

Brade looked at his watch. Nearly seven, and he couldn't leave even yet. Something had to be done first.

He closed the grimy Venetian blinds and put on the overhead fluorescents to add to the light of the desk lamp. The thick of the evening's extension courses had not yet begun, and the building was virtually empty. The clot of students and others who had gathered with the arrival of the police had dissolved with their departure.

He was grateful for that, for the privacy.

He had work to do quickly, and he badly needed all the privacy he could get.

2

IT was a long drive home, though not, perhaps, as clocks measure time. The unaccustomed darkness made the surroundings seem strange and wintery. The texture of the traffic was different. The polychrome reflection-blurs on the river, cast by the miscellaneous luminescence of the city, gave everything an air of unreality.

As unreal as his life, Brade thought.

A long escape, his life, nothing more. Four years in college during the slowly-lightening depression years, aided by NYA funds. (In those days, he thought bitterly, there was the flavor of charity about government help.

Nowadays, those students who needed money, at least in the physical sciences, could pick away at the various research grants with no loss of caste whatever. They could even be disdainful about the matter and shop from professor to professor without concealing the price tag on their services.)

Then, after the four years, despite the tremolo of the valedictory address and the muted bass of the presidential benediction, Brade did not leave the ivied halls to "face life." He simply changed universities; he changed hiding places.

It went by steps. The master's degree and the doctor's degree under Cap Anson, then a position on the faculty first as instructor and then as assistant professor.

And none of it was "Life." (He negotiated a traffic circle with the blind ease of one who has driven a car so long that it knows its own way home, smelling the garage from afar and hastening.)

A university was part of life in the sense that an eddy was part of a stream. The students were in the main current, sweeping in from the distant brooks and rivulets of childhood, coursing past, then leaving to follow the stream further through a land Brade had never explored. And Brade remained behind in the changeless academic eddy.

And while he did so, the students grew younger. They had been almost Brade's chronological equals in his first years as an instructor and the dignity of his own position had sat uncomfortably upon him. Now (how many years later was it? Good Lord, seventeen) he need grope for no dignity. The students found it in the texture of his face and the veins on his hand.

They professor-ed him and spoke politely. That was

the just due of one who grew older in a world of perpetual youth.

Yet even within the eddy of academic life, there were certain values that could be given more or less meaning on its own artificial and ingrown scale.

For instance, there was a magic boundary line facing Brade. It came between the rank of assistant professor, which Brade had held for eleven years, and the next higher rank of associate professor, of which Brade had been clearly deprived for at least three of those years.

His foot and the car's accelerator combined to move him on as a traffic light turned green.

The magic word "tenure" sat on that boundary line, and another word "security." On this side of the line, he was "assistant professor" and could be discharged at will for any cause, or no cause. His appointment need merely go unrenewed. It was as simple as that. On the other side, he was "associate professor" and could be discharged only for cause and very few excuses were "cause" enough. He would be safe for life. But now, because of what had happened to one of his students, that boundary line would recede once again, out of crossing distance.

His lips tightened as he turned into his own street. He could make out the lights of his own house ahead, broken up by the branches of the sycamore in the front yard.

Doris' concern would be, of course, for the fate of his promotion. He could hear himself assure her that he would not be held responsible for any of this.

If only, he thought, if only that were so.

Doris met him at the door. From the movement of the curtain at one living room window as his car moved into the driveway, Brade knew she had been watching for him.

He should have called, he thought, guiltily. Of course, he was late at times; it was no catastrophe in itself. Still—

As a matter of fact, he had (consciously, at that) tried to avoid talking to her. What did he say *now*, for God's sake?

Apologize for not calling? Talk rapidly on neutral subjects? Ask for Anson? What? .

It was like the time they had driven frozenly home from a department gathering of students and faculty at which he had been markedly attentive to one of the student's wives, one who obviously strove by dimples and decolletage to better her husband's chances. At that time, he recalled, he had entered the house and said in sheerest desperation, "Oh, hell, let's have a drink."

It had worked. Not a word was said, either that night, or next morning, or ever.

How about that, he wondered.

And it was all taken out of his hands when Doris stepped aside to let him cross the threshold and said, "I heard about it. How awful!"

She was almost as tall as he was and of darker coloring. Her face had not yet gone into fine lines with advancing middle age as his had. It remained as smooth about the eyes and lip-corners as when they were both in college. Instead, there had been a slight but definite hardening of outlines, a soft exterior tautening over a bony substructure.

Brade looked at her now as though he had never seen her before. "You *heard* about it? How? Don't tell me it was on—on TV?" He felt foolish, even as he asked that.

She closed the door behind him and said, "The secretary called."

"Jean Makris?"

"That's right. She told me what happened, that Ralph was dead. She said you'd probably be late and guessed you probably wouldn't feel like eating. She seemed quite concerned that I treat you gently and with understanding. Has she been told that I fall down in that respect?"

Brade shook off the irony. "All right, Doris. It's the way she is."

He flopped into the living-room armchair, dropping his topcoat over the arm and letting a sleeve drag on the floor. Ordinarily, he was extremely neat in trivial things (a neurosis he liked to blame on the requirements of chemical research, but which Doris attributed to the after-effects of a domineering mother).

He said, "Is Ginny in bed?"

"Oh, yes."

"She hasn't heard about it yet, has she?"

"Not yet." She picked up his coat and went to the hall closet with it and her voice came back a trifle muted. "Do you, Lou?"

"Do I what?"

"Feel like eating?"

"Good Lord, no. Couldn't think of it. At least, for a while."

"Then you'll have a drink." That was not a question.

And for once, Brade, no great drinker, had not even the impulse of objecting. (Suddenly, he wished Ginny had not been put to bed so uncommonly early. She would have been a breath of normality to him.)

Doris was at the built-in cupboard of the dining-room area, where they kept their undistinguished supply of liquor.

Brade watched her and wondered. Why did so many different things go so differently wrong? All his marriage long the world had faced atomic doom. All his childhood long his family had faced depression. Had he been carrying on in rubble all his life and not known it for rubble because it was all he knew?

Doris disappeared into the kitchen after the soda and ice and returned quickly with a drink for each of them. She sat down on the the hassock next to the armchair and stared levelly at him out of wide-set brown eyes (her best feature really, thought Brade).

She said, "How, exactly, did it happen? All I know so far is that it was some kind of accident."

Brade took care of half his drink at a sip. He coughed raggedly, but felt better. "Apparently, he used sodium cyanide where he should have used sodium acetate."

He did not bother to explain further than that. She was no chemist, but she had picked up some of the terminology just by associating with one as long and as closely as she had.

"Oh," she said. Then, with the line of her jaw showing squarely against the floor lamp, she went on, "It *is* too bad, Lou, but after all there isn't the shadow of responsibility on you for this thing, is there?"

Brade stared at his drink. "No, of course not." Then he said, "What did Cap Anson say when he came and didn't find me. I assume he was angry."

Doris gestured that away. "I didn't even see him. He spoke to Ginny outside."

"And too furious to come in. Huh."

Doris said, "Never mind Cap, now. What did Professor Littleby say?"

"Nothing, dear. He wasn't in."

"Well, that won't last. If all else fails, we'll be seeing him Saturday night."

Brade corrugated his forehead and didn't look at her. "You think we ought to go to that affair, Doris?"

"Of course, we'll go. It's just like any other year. Good Lord, Lou, it's very sad, but we're not going into mourning, are we?" She clicked her tongue once against her teeth. "That boy has brought only trouble to everyone."

"Now, Doris—"

"Otto Ranke told you that when you first took on Ralph."

"I don't think Ranke foresaw anything of this sort," said Brade quietly.

Ranke had been Ralph Neufeld's first choice as research professor. Usually, the choice lay with the student. He spoke to the various members of the department and selected that one whose field of research seemed most interesting. Or who had the most lavish list of government grants.

And Neufeld had selected Ranke.

But Ranke was a difficult choice. Ordinarily, a professor stuck with any student whom he had accepted, and though he might be sorry afterward, he felt it was his duty to see him through to Ph.D. or to irremediable failure.

Professor Otto Ranke, however, felt bound by no such self-limiting rule. When a student proved personally unsatisfactory to him, he drove the youngster from his presence with loud cries.

He was the ranking physical chemist of the department, a short, plump man with tufts of white hair around each ear and a pink desert between; rich in awards and honors and the department's outstanding possibility for a Nobel Prize some day.

His ill-humor and outspokenness were proverbial, though Brade always felt there was a certain deliberateness behind the sneers and tantrums. The temperament of genius, after all, was easy enough to assume and, probably, came with especial ease to those with vague suspicions that the actuality was more elusive.

In any case, Neufeld, whose own ill-humor made no allowances for the ill-humor of even the most powerful, came to the parting of the ways with his professor inside of a month. At once, he approached Brade and suggested a transfer of allegiance.

Brade, as a matter of routine, questioned Ranke concerning the youngster, and was greeted with an indignant snort. "The boy is impossible. One can't work with him. He brings trouble everywhere."

Brade smiled. "You're not exactly easy to work with yourself, Otto."

"It has nothing to do with me," said Ranke, vehemently. "He got into a fist-fight, an actual fist-fight, with August Winfield."

"What about?"

"Some foolishness about Winfield using a beaker that Neufeld had just cleaned. Now I never had any trouble with Winfield before, and he's a promising enough boy. I'm not going to have a psychotic disrupt my group. If you accept him, Lou, he'll make trouble for you."

But Brade had ignored that. He had put the boy into a laboratory by himself for a while, dealt with him gently and distantly, and hung on. He was aware of the reputation he had for picking up the personality-problem student that the other professors tried to avoid, and he even felt a sneaking pride in the reputation.

At times he almost honestly forgot that his own lack of grants brought him only the odd ones in the first place.

And at that, some of his specimens turned out first-class researchers who proved well worth any difficulties they might have caused. Spencer James, Brade's prize sample, was with Manning Chemicals and doing very well—better than most of Ranke's pliant and clean-cut hoop-jumpers.

Neufeld, after a very slow start, had shown definite promise of becoming a prize of his own. His recent data had been both startling and heartening, and there had been every sign that within half a year, he and Brade would have been able to prepare a most satisfactory dissertation.

The momentary little daydream grew, flowered, and shattered, all in the split-second of thought that had followed Doris' reference to Ranke. But there was no dissertation, after all, only cyanide.

Brade said, following out his thought, "In a way, I *should* be in mourning. Ralph Neufeld was a whiz at mathematics; much better than I could possibly be. Together, we could have put out a paper that might have placed in the *Journal of Chemical Physics*; a nice mathematical one that would have lit up the inside of Littleby's skull and set it whizzing."

"Get someone else to finish up," said Doris at once.

"I could persuade the new student, Simpson, to take Ranke's course in kinetics and carry on, I suppose, but I don't know that Simpson can carry the course. Besides, just finishing the last strokes of a problem won't get Simpson a doctorate and I'm responsible for seeing that he gets one."

"You're responsible to yourself also, Lou. And to your family, don't forget that."

Brade swirled the drop of liquid remaining at the bottom of his glass. How was he going to tell her?

The decision was postponed for a bit by the sound of a scrabbling noise of bare feet on carpet in the upper hall. A girl's voice called, shrilly, "Daddy. You home? Daddy?"

Doris walked purposefully to the stairs and called out with a kind of controlled force, "Virginia—"

But Brade interposed. "Let me talk to her."

Doris said, "Cap Anson gave her a couple of chapters to give to you. That's all she has to say."

"Well, I'll talk to her, anyway." He climbed the stairs. "What's up, Ginny?"

He squatted down and hugged her. She would be twelve her next birthday.

Ginny said, "Well, I *thought* I heard you come home, and you didn't come up to say good-night after Mother just *made* me go to bed right after supper, so I came out to see."

"I'm glad you did, Ginny."

"And I have a message for you." In a few more years, Ginny would be as tall as her mother and she already had her mother's dark, smooth hair and wide-set brown eyes. Her skin was fair, though, as fair as her father's.

Ginny said, "Cap Anson stopped by when I was outside—"

"At just five o'clock." (Brade grinned gently. He knew the old man's obsessive punctuality and felt shame once again at having failed him. Yet it wasn't his fault; it simply *wasn't*.)

"Yes," said Ginny, "and he gave me an envelope and said to give it to you when you came home."

"And he seemed angry."

"He stood sort of stiff; and he didn't smile or anything."

"And do you have the envelope?"

"Here it is." She went flying and returned with a bulging manila envelope. "I kept it for you."

"Thank you very much, Ginny. And now you'd better go back to bed. And close your door."

Ginny said, "All right," and picked idly at a band-aid that decorated her left wrist. "You and mamma talking privately?"

"Well, we don't want to disturb you. So I want your door closed."

He rose, feeling the slight creak in his knees, and tucked Cap Anson's manuscript under his arm. But Ginny stared at him with eager brightness in her eyes. "Is there trouble at the University, Daddy?"

Brade felt uneasy. Had she been listening? He said, "Why do you ask, Ginny?"

She seemed definitely excited and troubled. "Did P'fessor Littleby *fire* you?"

Brade sucked in his breath, then said sharply, "Now that was silly, young lady. You march into your room. No one's firing Daddy. Go ahead, now go ahead."

Ginny retreated. Her door closed but not entirely and Brade advanced to slam it shut. "And not another sound from you," he called out.

He went down the stairs at a quiet boil. It was no use being angry with Ginny. Rather, he should have consoled her. If she had picked up her parents' insecurities, the fault lay with the elders.

It decided him against trying to find a mild and antiseptic way of breaking the news to Doris. Let her face it, he thought angrily.

He faced her squarely and said, "The real trouble,

Doris, is just this. Ralph Neufeld's death was no accident."

She looked shocked. "You mean he did it purposely? He killed himself?"

"No. Why should he set up a complete experiment just to kill himself? I mean, he was killed by someone else. He was murdered."

3

DORIS stared at her husband, laughed angrily, and said, "You're crazy, Lou—" She choked herself off and her eyes widened. "Were the police there? Did *they* say so?"

"Of course the police were there. It was a violent death. But no, they didn't say so. They think it's an accident."

"Well, then, suppose you leave it to them."

"They don't know enough, Doris. They're not chemists."

"What has that to do with it?"

Brade looked vaguely at his fingers, then reached up to put out the floorlamp. His head was beginning to throb and he found its light unpleasant. A soft twilight reached the room from the kitchen fluorescents and that was much better.

He said, "Sodium acetate and sodium cyanide might be

in identical bottles and Ralph might have grabbed hold of the wrong one and not noticed. That's possible. But still he would not have been fooled."

"Why not?"

"If you were to try it, you would see. To the detective on the case, both chemicals seemed white and crystalline and that was enough for him. But that's not all there is and heaven knows I didn't encourage him to do more than look. The two substances aren't alike. They pack differently. The sodium acetate absorbs atmospheric moisture more than the cyanide does, so the crystals clump together more. A chemist used to taking out acetate with a spatula, as Ralph was, could tell there was something wrong as soon as he dug into the cyanide, even if he were blindfolded."

Doris sat on the couch across from him, a quiet, menacing figure in the dimness. Her hands were a patch of white against the darkness of her dress. She said, "Have you been telling anyone this?"

"No."

"I wouldn't have been surprised if you had. You have your odd moments; and this time you're more than odd. I think you're mad."

"Why mad?"

"Now, look, Littleby as much as promised you'd get your associate professorship this year. You said so."

"I didn't quite say so, dear. I said he told me that eleven years were quite enough to wait. For all I know that might mean he was ready to ask for my resignation—or fire me, as Ginny said. I suppose you know she thought I had been fired."

Doris took it stolidly. "I heard her."

"Why should she think such a thing?"

"I suppose because she heard us speaking of the matter. She's not deaf, and she's old enough to understand what she hears."

"Do you think it's right to fill her with insecurity?"

"No wronger than to fill her with false security. Don't get off the subject, Lou. You will have to get tenure."

Brade's voice trembled slightly but remained low. "The subject is murder, Doris."

"The subject is your rank. With one of your students poisoned, Littleby is quite capable of using that as an excuse to withhold promotion. And if you go about talking of *murder* and creating a scandal, why it would settle matters for you."

"I have no intention of—" began Brade.

"I know you'll *intend* to be discreet, but then you'll begin to feel it your duty to do something ridiculous. Your duty to the school or to society. Your damned duty to everyone but to your family."

"I think you're not thinking this through, Doris," said Brade. The one thing he did not want this evening was a lecture. "If there's a murderer on the campus, I can't just ignore that. A chemistry laboratory is the last place where you dare leave a murderer free. Using cyanide is one way of killing, but if he takes it into his head to kill again, there are a hundred ways, a thousand. You couldn't guard against them all even if forewarned. Is it my duty to my family to expose myself as a possible victim?"

"Why you, for Heaven's sake."

"Why anyone? Why Ralph? Why not myself the next time?"

"Oh, put on the light." She did that herself, with an impatient snap of the wrist. "You are the most exasperating person. *What* murder? Your idiot student *did* take the cyanide and didn't notice. That's the fact, and you can't make the fact disappear by talk. He was distracted and didn't notice. It's easy to say that no chemist would mistake cyanide for acetate, but that assumes a chemist is a perfect machine. A chemist can be thoughtless, distracted, sleepy, angry, anxious. He can make any number of mistakes, even ridiculous ones. Well, Ralph did exactly that."

Brade shook his head. The light bothered him but he made no move to turn it out again. He said, "It's not just that, Doris. There is material evidence." He spoke slowly, consciously choosing his words to make sure she understood. "Ralph was methodical, and he always got reaction components ready in advance as far as possible so that he never had to interrupt an experiment to get something that wasn't at hand. He was a most meticulous worker. For instance, he prepared sodium acetate in two-gram lots in each of ten Erlenmeyer flasks and that carried him through one series of experiments.

"After the detective left, I looked in his desk and found seven of the Erlenmeyers still remaining. The contents looked like sodium acetate, but I tested them with silver nitrate solution, since looks aren't enough. If cyanide were present in even tiny amounts, there would have been a white precipitate of silver cyanide as the first drop of nitrate solution struck. But there was nothing.

"Then I found the flask that Ralph had used in his last experiment. It was standing in the hood just behind his reaction set-up. It hadn't been completely emptied. It didn't have to be since the amount of acetate added wasn't the rate-determining step, so there were a number of crystals adhering to the glass. I dissolved them, added the silver nitrate, and got the precipitate.

"Of course, the powder might have been ordinary salt,

sodium chloride, or some allied material. Silver chloride will also show up as a white precipitate, but silver chloride will not redissolve when the tube is swirled. Silver cyanide will, and this precipitate did. I suppose it's luck Doheny felt out of his depth and didn't really go into matters searchingly."

Doris said, sharply, "Doheny?"

"The detective."

"Oh. Well, then, if you don't mind my asking, what does all this rigmarole about Erlenmeyer flasks and silver nitrate mean?"

"Look, dear, it should be obvious to you. Ralph started with a series of ten flasks, all prepared at the same time. He used two of them, one yesterday, one the day before, and they didn't hurt him. It was the third that killed him. The seven that remained were harmless.

"Now if Ralph had mistaken sodium cyanide for sodium acetate—we'll say he was on edge, his nerves were shot, he didn't know what he was doing, anything you like—he would have filled every one of the flasks with cyanide. He would *not* have filled one, then gone back to the shelf like a zombie and gotten the acetate for the others. Nor would he have filled nine with acetate and then suddenly gone away to get cyanide for the tenth, by accident."

Doris frowned. "He might have started with cyanide and noticed his mistake."

"Then he would have emptied and cleaned the flask he had filled."

"He might have filled more than one, all ten maybe, and then overlooked one in the emptying."

"Now you want *two* unbelievable oversights. Mistaking cyanide for acetate is one; and then forgetting to empty a cyanide-filled flask is two. Good God, you don't fool around with a cyanide; even a chemist who's used to the stuff doesn't. He less than anyone, in fact. A chemist just couldn't be *that* distracted. They don't make distraction that complete. And Ralph was an extremely careful worker."

Doris said nothing and for a while after Brade finished there was a silence in which the chemist's thoughts rang hollowly. It was frightening the way in which one could start with so little and end with such consequence. And yet it was done as a matter of everyday routine in scientific research. Why should he be made so uneasy by the application to people of the logical system he did not hesitate to apply to symbols and atoms? The nature of the conclusions, perhaps.

Brade said, slowly, "The conclusion is that someone deliberately substituted cyanide for acetate in one of the flasks."

Doris said, "But why?"

"To kill Ralph, naturally."

"But why?"

"I don't know why. I don't know anything about the personal life of the boy, so how can I tell what motives might exist? He's been working with me for more than a year and a half and yet I know practically nothing about him."

"Do you feel guilt about that, too? What did Cap Anson know about you when you were working with him?"

Brade couldn't help but smile. Professor Anson, who in living memory seemed never to have been called anything but Cap for no reason that anyone could put their finger on (Brade seemed to recall a baseball player by the name of Cap Anson once; perhaps it was that), had thought any minute out of his lab a precious minute irretrievably lost; any conversation not dealing with some matter of research a mere thing of triviality and small talk.

He knew his students only as extensions of himself. Added arms, subsidiary minds.

Brade said, "Cap is a special case."

"Right now," said Doris, "I wish you'd be more like him. You always told me his big gift was the capacity never to go one step further than the facts allowed. You, instead, are just *galloping* ahead of the facts. Your whole theory is based on the supposition that Ralph prepared all ten flasks of acetate at once. How do you know he did? Even if he always did, how can you say that this time was not an exception?

"It's easy to say he was meticulous, Lou, and very careful, and all that; that he always did things just so. But people aren't machines, Lou. Even if he had a number of flasks standing in the cupboard, Ralph might still have wanted to make up an extra one for some reason we might not even be able to guess at, or for no reason at all. Maybe he split one or spoiled one or suddenly noticed he had only made up nine to begin with or—or anything. Then if he made up an extra one, just one, and used it, he might have gotten hold of the cyanide instead for that one, just that one."

Brade nodded wearily. "He might have and he may have and he could have. It's all subjunctive, all *ad hoc*. If we don't go to the trouble of inventing possibilities and maybes but just stick to the line of maximum probability, it ends up as murder."

Doris said in a low, controlled voice, "You're not going to start that, Lou. I don't care if it *is* murder. I don't want you stirring up any scandal. You're not to risk your tenure. Understand?"

The telephone rang a sudden summons. It was at Doris' hand and she took it. She looked up at him, hand over mouthpiece. "Professor Littleby."

Brade whispered in surprise. "What's up?"

She shook her head, and put a finger to her lips. "Careful."

Brade put the receiver to his ear. "Hello, Professor Littleby."

The other's voice, as it always did, brought up his face in clear and etched detail—its ruddy coloring, ruddier for the topping of pure white hair, the broad soft-jowled face, chin and nose equally smooth and equally bulbous (as though the creating angel in a momentary desire to save time had used the same mold for both) and white-fringed china-blue eyes.

The department head said, "Hello, Brade. Horrible affair. Just heard about it."

"Yes, sir. It was very unfortunate."

"I don't know much about the boy. I seem to recall some reservation about allowing him to go on for his doctorate, but of course that's neither here nor there now. Still character counts for a lot, and I have always noted that a tendency toward accidents in the laboratory correlates well with unsatisfactory personality. Dare say the psychiatrists would have fancy explanations, but I'm satisfied to observe facts. Uh, would you drop in before class tomorrow morning and see me?"

"Certainly, sir. May I ask what you wish to see me about?"

"Oh, just a consideration of some of the problems this brings up. You lecture at nine, don't you?"

"Yes, sir."

"Suppose you see me at 8:30 then. Well, Brade, bear up. Horrible. Horrible." And breaking a third "horrible" in two, he hung up.

"He wants to see you?" said Doris as soon as he turned away from the phone. "What about?"

"That he wouldn't say precisely." Brade picked up his long-empty glass and felt an impulse to fill it again. He said, instead, "I suppose we had better eat. Or have you eaten already?"

"No," she said, shortly.

They sat down over a salad, and for a while silence prevailed and Brade was thankful.

But Doris said, finally, "I want you to understand something, Lou."

"Yes, dear?"

"I'm not going to wait any longer. You must have tenure this year. If you do anything to spoil that, it's the end. I've waited a long time, Lou, and I've sat it out each June, waiting for you to get your little card announcing your appointment as assistant professor was renewed for one more year. I will not do that even one more June."

"You don't really think they won't renew it."

"I don't want to have to think about it at all. I don't want to weigh probabilities. I want certainty. If you're an associate professor, renewal is automatic. That's what tenure means, doesn't it, automatic renewal?"

"Except for cause."

"All right. I want June to mean nothing to me. I want fiscal years to mean nothing. I want tenure."

"I can't guarantee it, Doris," said Brade, mildly.

"You will *un*-guarantee it if you tell Littleby or anyone

of your crazy notions about murder. And if so, Lou—oh, Lou," her eyes blinked rapidly as though to hold back the tears, "I *can't* keep on like this."

Brade knew. He felt as she did. The scar marked them both. The depression years had gouged the courage out of each of them—the years of watching one's parents sick with anxiety; of knowing, somehow, but without quite understanding—

They wanted "tenure" to cure that memory, but what could he do?

Slowly and neatly, Brade cut through a leaf of lettuce with the side of his fork, halved the piece, then quartered it. He said, "I can't let go the matter as easily as you think. If it's murder, the police may eventually find that out."

"Let them. As long as you're not in it."

Brade said, "How can I not be in it?" He got to his feet. "I'm fixing myself another drink."

"Go ahead."

He mixed one clumsily and said, "Have you thought who the murderer might be, Doris?"

"No, I haven't. And I don't intend to."

"Well, think about it." He stared at her over the liquor, unhappy at having to face her with it, yet not knowing how to prevent it. "The murderer would have to be someone familiar with chemistry. Someone without experience in a laboratory wouldn't dare gimmick an experiment in order to bring about death by cyanide. He wouldn't feel sufficient confidence. He would have to rely on something less esoteric; a gun, a knife, a push from a height."

"Are you implying now that you think the murderer is a member of the department?"

"He must be. Someone must have come into the lab

and substituted cyanide for the acetate in one of the
flasks. It could hardly have been done while Ralph was in
the laboratory. For one thing, Ralph was a morbidly suspicious fellow who would allow no one near his equipment; it was that very fact that got him into trouble with
Ranke. So the substitution would have to be arranged
when Ralph was absent. And when Ralph left the lab he
always locked up, even when he was just going down to
the library to check a reference. I've seen him do that a
number of times. So the murderer would have to be someone with a key."

"Oh, these deductions," said Doris. "Just because
you've seen him lock up, doesn't mean he invariably did.
Sometimes, he might have forgotten. And even if he never
forgot, keys aren't the only ways to open locks."

"Maybe, if you want to consider fringe probabilities.
But consider the most likely interpretation, not the least
likely ones. Work it out the way the police probably will.
It would have to be someone with a key and someone
who would know the nature of Ralph's experiments, know
where he kept his acetate flasks and so on. Moreover,
only one of the flasks was substituted."

"Why," asked Doris, finally caught up.

"Because the murderer knew Ralph's meticulous
nature. He would have counted on Ralph's using the
flasks from the left hand side and running precisely one
experiment each day. That would make the poisoned one
come up on a Thursday when Ralph would be alone in
the laboratory because his roommate would be in the
classroom. And no cyanide would be left over to endanger
others. The murderer was right at home with the necessary conditions."

"What are you getting at, Lou?"

"Just that the police will list all these requirements, too, and find the one person that best fits them."

"Who?"

"Who! Why do you suppose I was so careful to avoid even hinting any of this to the police?" Brade sipped carefully at his drink, then, on impulse, tossed it off. He said, thickly, "Myself, my dear. I am the one likely suspect that fits all the facts. The only possible suspect."

4

THE drive to the university next morning seemed longer than had the drive home the night before. He had topped the evening with a third drink and finally a fourth and had been dazed rather than cheered for his pains.

Doris had maintained an ominous silence that had reduced her to an unbending session of television-watching. Brade had tried to slip Cap Anson's chapters out of their envelope and give them a light once-over for the old man's sake, but the type twirled madly and after reading the initial paragraph five times, he gave up.

Neither one of them slept afterward and in the morning Ginny had slipped off to school with a tense and frightened look on her thin face. Children, Brade had long since decided, had invisible antennae that vibrated to the moods of the unpredictable adults that made up their lives.

Not that he blamed Doris, or himself for that matter. It was all the result of a tangle of circumstance that caught at the stumbling feet of all humanity.

He had been finishing his Ph.D. research under old Cap (old Cap, even then) when he had received an offer of an instructorship at the university beginning the next July 1. It was heaven-sent; it was all that the wildest dreams could ask for. He didn't want the excitement—and insecurity—of industry. He wasn't made for the cheerful push over the next fellow's tripped torso. He didn't even want the push for grants. He wanted only the quiet sure position. Security, not adventure.

It was then he married Doris. She wanted what he wanted; the unassuming sureness of next year. They would sacrifice the rise of the rocket in order to be sure of missing forever the fall of the stick.

And what could be better than a faculty position in a hoary old university? Depression might come and salaries might even be temporarily cut, but faculty members survived and survived into the days of whiskered reverence. And even when they retired it was upon the soft cushion of half-pay emeritus status, until the final attendance record was taken and the professor could lift his weary eyes at last to that great big blackboard in the sky.

Time passed, two years of it, and he was an assistant professor. His research was in odd corners—interesting but quiet. There was no hurly-burly even there for he chose his projects to avoid that. The research grants went to the hurly-burly, however, and those grants passed him by. And so did the associate professorship.

He could understand how Doris felt about it. Seventeen

years on the job and each year there was the white slip—
not a pink slip, but a white slip—announcing renewal of
appointment. For one year.

Naturally, Doris wanted tenure.

Brade tried to explain that tenure was only a word.
That it meant you could not be fired except for cause and
by vote of the university senate (composed of fellow professors jealously guarding their own tenure), but that no
professor *need* be fired. One could, instead, be asked in a
polite whisper to resign and if one did not, but chose to
stay, the petty irritations of each day could be made to
mount sky-high until, tenure or not, resignation would be
rubbed into the skin and made to stick.

But Doris knew only that this way, the way it was now,
all they need do was fail to include the little white slip.
Without tenure, no cause was needed, no vote.

It was Depression-disease. She wanted security.

He wanted it, too, Brade thought somberly.

He pulled into the faculty parking lot and took an open
space. He took what he could get. The reserved places
against the stone back wall of the chemistry building were
for associate and full professors. Ordinarily, he didn't pay
mind to that, but suddenly, that, too, was an aspect of the
security that went with the magic dividing line.

He walked up the open-work wooden staircase that
took him around the building to the upper-level main entrance in front. A pair of students on one of the stone
benches lining the bricked walk across the lawn, looked
up at him. One whispered to the other and their eyes followed him.

Brade hunched his shoulders and walked on. He hadn't

bought the paper that morning. Doubtless it carried the story.

Well, did that make him a curiosity, for God's sake? Did the death's head show through the skin of his face? Was there a sign: cyanide, beware?

He found himself striding at a ridiculous pace and forced his steps to slow as he walked through the large double door.

And just turning left at that point made the day begin wrong. He should turn right toward the elevator which would take him to the fourth floor and his office.

But he turned left and entered the one with DEPARTMENT OF CHEMISTRY on the door, and suddenly he felt himself back in grade school again with a stern teacher seven feet tall having sent him to see the eight-foot principal.

He looked at his watch. It was 8:20 and he was ten minutes early.

Jean Makris got rid of a student and rose as Brade took a seat.

She said, "He'll be with you in a minute, Professor Brade. He's on the phone right now."

"That's all right," said Brade. "I'm early."

She walked from behind her desk and through the swinging horizontal bar that served in the office as a gate and came to him, all trouble. Brade restrained the tendency to shy away, but it always seemed to him on these occasions that she was about to straighten his tie.

She was a long-faced girl with prominent teeth and a mournful expression, not necessarily related, Brade thought, to any sadness within. She was efficient, shunted unwelcome visitors away expertly, kept him informed of appointments and substituted in what time she had and as best she could for the secretary of his own that the school would not finance.

She said, confidentially, "I was terribly upset when you called me yesterday, Professor Brade. You must have felt awful."

"It was quite a shock, Miss Makris."

She grew even more confidential. "I hope Mrs. Brade understood about you being late. I tried to explain."

"Yes. Thank you."

"I just figured that with you so punctual and all, Mrs. Brade might think, you know—She might be upset and get to thinking, you know—"

Brade wondered for a wild moment if Miss Makris were hinting of possible suspicions of sexual irregularities. He stared at her with a kind of horror.

She switched the main weight of topic smoothly. "I suppose you're especially upset because he's your student."

"Yes. One might say that."

"Well, in that connection—"

A soft buzzer sounded on Miss Makris's desk and she said at once, "Professor Littleby will see you now—but I'll tell you when you come out." She nodded earnestly at him.

His last sight of her was as she adjusted her white blouse, as virginally white, on doubt, Brade thought idly, as the inconspicuous bosom that heaved beneath it.

Professor Littleby put down his phone as Brade entered and smiled mechanically.

There might have been a time, Brade thought, when that smile had been a real thing, but people in high administrative position can scarcely rely on human motivation to produce smiles on all proper occasions. They need something more reliable and more unfailing, so that machinery is installed and lubricated until the smile is guaranteed to flit across the face at all proper moments, however unmoved the fact itself or the mind behind it might be.

Brade said, with a mechanical smile of his own, "Good morning, Professor Littleby."

Professor Littleby nodded, rubbed his ear and said, "Terrible thing. Terrible thing."

His broad face, shaven into ruddy gleaming smoothness, reflected the trouble for an appropriate moment. He wore a jacket, of course, but a vest underneath that too. He was the only member of the faculty who persisted in wearing a vest at all seasons, whether out of an appreciation of his administrative position or an honest ignorance at its passing from the masculine scene, Brade did not know.

Time had stopped for Littleby these last twenty years. Back then, his book on electrochemistry had been in its third edition and had been the standard text in the field. But no fourth edition had ever come, and it was now out of print. Occasionally, Littleby talked wistfully of preparing a new edition if he ever found the time, but even he himself did not really believe it.

It didn't matter. The book had made his reputation and a few patents involving the electroplating of chromium had brought him a moderate but independent income and the offer of the department headship when old Bannerman had died.

Brade nodded and agreed that it was a terrible thing.

"Of course," said Littleby, "it is somehow not surprising that it should happen to that particular student. Quite a misfit, as I said on the phone last night. I've been checking the faculty reports on him and I am sorry to have to say it about your student since you have reported him as doing well, but the faculty members generally thought little of him."

"He was a difficult young man in some ways," said Brade, "but he had his virtues."

"I dare say," said Littleby, coldly. "However, that is beside the point. My chief concern must be for the school, for the department."

Littleby adjusted the papers on his desk and Brade watched him cautiously.

"We can't have it said," Littleby went on, "that due precautions weren't taken; that safety was neglected."

"No, of course not."

"How did it happen, by the way? I understand it was hydrogen cyanide, but how did he come to breathe it?"

Brade explained the surface facts only.

Littleby said, "Well, there you are. It should not have been an open system. There should have been a reflux condenser on the vessel. That would have kept his foolish nose out of the way."

Brade wanted to say at that point that he himself had suggested a reflux condenser to Ralph more than once, but that would have seemed like hiding behind a corpse. He satisfied himself by saying, "It would have meant special equipment, sir, and I think that Neufeld thought that he would retain better control of the conditions of the experiment if he left the vessel open. Vapor loss was not crucial and he could add material with less wasted motion."

"Nonsense. The trouble with youngsters these days is

that safety comes last with them. I tell you I've gone through the labs and I've been sickened, *sickened* at what I've seen. I've watched solvents being boiled over an open flame. Nobody seems to use an asbestos gauze when heating. And the hoods are in terrible condition. Frankly, I was intending to call a department meeting to consider that very point and the fact that I did not do it before this happened is very distressing to me."

Brade moved uneasily in his chair. There was nothing unreasonably wrong with the safety precautions in the student laboratories. "Sir, this has been the only accident past a cut finger or an acid burn in ten years."

"How many accidents like this do you *want?*"

Brade was silent, and Littleby, savoring his weightily-delivered retort for a few moments, then went on, "Now I think what we ought to do is to organize a class on safety, a series of lectures on the do's and dont's of the chemical way of life, so to speak. They can be held at five in the afternoon and the attendance will be compulsory for all students, graduate and undergraduate, taking any of the chemistry lab courses. What do you think?"

"We can try it out."

"Good. I'll ask you, Professor Brade, to organize the course, and I think it would be a good idea if you asked Cap Anson to join you. The old gentleman would be happy to be active, I know, and this would be a good opportunity to arrange something for him."

Brade said coldly, "Yes, sir."

He didn't like this. It seemed arranged as a punishment for him, a Dantesque expiation, a purification ritual. His student had been careless and as a result he must force other students to be less careless.

Littleby said, "A lecture a week, perhaps, and I'd start

this week. If the newspapers—" He cleared his throat. "It wouldn't hurt, I suppose, to say we'd been planning this for quite a while as part of our continuing safety program. And it wouldn't be untrue, either, for as I've been telling you, the subject had been on my mind. Yes."

He looked suddenly at the clock on the wall, which stood at a quarter of nine. "Your class is at nine, isn't it, Professor Brade?"

"Yes, it is."

"I suppose you feel up to taking it. Conceivably, this might have upset you to the point where—"

"It hasn't," said Brade, quickly. "I am perfectly ready to lecture."

"Good, good. Oh, as for my little get-together tomorrow night. Your good wife and yourself will still be able to attend, I hope? Though if you feel that under the circumstances—"

Brade had trouble keeping the stiffness out of his voice, "I think we'll come. We find the occasion so pleasant that—"

And each, in a welter of trailing sentences, nodded stiffly and smiled mechanically at each other, with a courtesy drained and desiccated of all amiability.

He doesn't want me to come, thought Brade. I'm touched by death. Bad publicity.

If it weren't for Doris, we wouldn't come.

Poor Doris. If there were a chance for promotion before, it looked rather desperate now. There was no largesse gleaming in Littleby's rather small eyes. Poor himself. Would Doris manage to bear it? She sometimes talked desperately but she had found hidden reserves before and surely she would again.

Another thought of another kind came to him as he

turned and walked out of the office. It was based on Littleby's remark about the faculty reports. Each lecturer, in addition to marking the student with a letter grade that was made public, reported, as far as he could, on the character and personality of the student. The latter was kept private.

It was available, of course, to the faculty, and Brade had glanced over the comments on Ralph, as a matter of course, when first considering him as a Ph.D. student. It had been just that, however—a glance. He knew at the time that Ralph was not well thought of and so he discounted the judgments.

Now a new aspect was placed upon the whole matter. Whoever killed the boy must have felt something for him; hate, anger, something; strong enough to result in murder.

Ranke disliked the boy intensely, of course, and even Dr. Shulter of the medical school, who had met him only casually, disapproved of him, and so might almost all. But there could be something in the wording of one man's judgment that might betray something additional, some little extra touch of emotion.

At any rate, Brade thought with strong relief, his own statements about Ralph had been largely complimentary. He was the one faculty member against whom dislike to one degree or another, flowing between Ralph and himself, could not be shown.

"Eh?" He was startled, as sound penetrated past his eardrums, finally. "I'm sorry, Miss Makris. I'm afraid I wasn't listening."

"You certainly weren't," said Jean Makris, roguishly. "You came out of the office in a real brown study, and I had to grab your elbow or I think you would have walked into the door."

"Yes. Well, I'm all right now."

"Professor Littleby wasn't—" her eyes slid furtively in the direction of the inner door, "nasty or anything, was he?"

"No, it was quite a routine conference."

"That's good. Well, then, I'll just tell you, to ease your mind, you know, in case you're all upset about Ralph; in case you feel a personal loss, kind of—"

She was staring at him earnestly, now, her long face tilted a little to one side and there was something lively in her voice as though she had been waiting to say this thing a long time, yet didn't want to spoil the experience by a too-rapid consummation.

Brade said, "I have a class now, Miss Makris. Exactly what is it you're trying to say?"

Her face was suddenly close to his, her eyes gleaming. "Just that Ralph was no good. Just that you needn't feel bad about him. He *hated* you."

5

BRADE hastened from her without a word, walking rapidly up the stairs in automatic haste toward his office. Between the second and third floors he remembered that his class was about to start, turned suddenly and hastened down again.

He entered the first-floor amphitheater somewhat short of breath. The class had already assembled.

The room was a large one and the most old-fashioned and bulky of the altogether old-fashioned and bulky chemistry building. Its seats were banked with increasing steepness toward the rear of the room so that the two aisles were equipped with shallow steps. The seats in the last few rows swept around and along the sides of the room to form a balcony.

The room as a whole would seat 250, which made it suitable for seminars and for tests during which students could be made to sit well separated. The undergraduate organic class, however, contained sixty-four students and, generally, they formed a moderate conglomeration in the central section near the podium and scattered off backward and to each side.

There was no formal seating arrangement so that this spontaneous self-seating could, Brade thought, be treated mathematically as a problem in diffusion.

He had also observed that in general it was the poorer students who sat farthest away. Now why was that? Was it that they hoped to go unnoticed? That they sought, with unconscious humility, a separation from their superior fellows? That they found the lecturer dull and offensive and strove to make the sound of him dimmer by distance?

There was a subject for research by scholars interested in human behavior. (And sometimes, when he thought this, Brade would feel a wash of envy. The social scientists had not the same hard intellectual discipline to contend with as did the physical scientists. They had a field of research that was soft and uncertain. They could be scholars in the old-fashioned sense, whereas physical scientists had been thrown out into the ice-world of international politics and pressing human needs. A social scientist could study the relationship of a student's marks to his position in a classroom and would require no fancy instruments to do so and there would be no pressure on him to prove that his research had some connection with cancer, heart-disease, or rocket-fuels in order that he might get a government subsidy for it.)

Of course, on this particular day, the seating arrangement differed markedly from the norm. There was no diffusion. The sixty-four students had gathered in a dense knot compressed into the section nearest the podium as though a giant hand had applied pressure from the rear and squeezed.

Louis Brade, from his position on the raised lecture platform, could not resist adjusting his glasses as though this might be some sort of optical illusion.

They want to watch my face, he thought. They want to see how I feel now that one of my students has died.

Or was it just the general fascination of death?

He began lecturing in the dry and level voice he reserved for these occasions. "Today we begin the consideration of several important groups of compounds characterized by the presence in their molecules of a carbon and oxygen connected by a double bond. This is called a carbonyl group."

He drew the carbonyl group on the board.

His voice sounded unshaken in his own ears, normal, unaffected by events. For once he was thankful for his own peculiar lecturing style which deliberately suppressed the intrusion of his own personality.

It was the antithesis, for instance, of the style affected by Merrill Foster, the other organic chemist of the department (seven years at his job, equally an assistant professor along with Brade, bright, ambitious—and a showman).

Foster taught the graduate course in synthetic organic chemistry; that is, the course for those students who, having graduated college, were working toward advanced degrees in chemistry. Brade could never think of that without a quick memory of the day Foster had been appointed to organize that course and Doris' violent reaction to the news.

It had been difficult to explain to Doris that the undergraduate course was the more demanding and responsible of the two. The graduate course had an attendance of fifteen rather than sixty-four. Foster lectured three times a week, rather than the five a week Brade had to devote to the undergraduate course.

But Doris saw fewer lectures and fewer students as making it an easier job rather than a less responsible one. And at the same time she saw it as a more important job as though a lecturer in a graduate course reached a higher status than a lecturer in an undergraduate course through reflection from the comparative status of the respective students.

Actually, Brade told Doris, it was always the older and more experienced members of the department who were entrusted with the undergraduates. Any young squirt fresh out of Ph.D. work could handle graduate students.

And, at that, Brade rather disapproved of Foster's methods of handling. Foster lectured in a bright and deliberately colloquial manner which pleased some students but which also weakened discipline. Foster referred to the useless material prepared by side-reactions in the course of a synthesis as "gunk" or "crud." He never added pyridine; he always gave a reaction a "squirt of pyridine."

What seemed worse to Brade was that Foster interspersed his lectures with disparaging remarks about students in general and, usually, about some one student in particular—some student, preferably, who could be goaded into answering back and made to engage in a duel of wits between podium and back seat; a duel which podium could always win.

Brade went on, "The carbon atom of the carbonyl group, you will notice, has two unfulfilled valence bonds which can, most simply, be filled by a pair of hydrogen atoms. In that case, the compound that results is formaldehyde."

Strange how he could lecture and yet feel his mind working busily underneath. It reminded him of the old joke of the old professor who said, "Last night I dreamed I was lecturing to my class. I woke suddenly, and by God, sir, I *was*."

Ralph Neufeld had done badly in Foster's course, ending with a C. Brade had tried to discuss the matter with him but had been greeted with a stubborn silence broken only by the student's glowering statement of personal dislike for Foster.

At the time, Brade thought he knew what might have happened. Ralph was the type of victim Foster could not possibly have resisted and Ralph was simply not the kind to sit still under the lash. If Foster had made him the butt of some comments, Ralph would be bound to reply in kind and perhaps more bitingly than Foster would have anticipated.

It was hard to say what influence personal antagonism

would have on the mark but Brade decided he would have to pay particular attention to Foster's comments concerning Ralph in the faculty reports.

"The term, aldehyde, used as generic name for those compounds containing a carbonyl group to which at least one hydrogen atom is directly attached, is derived from the term 'alcohol dehydrogenated' by taking the first syllable of the first word and the first two syllables of the second. As you can plainly see, an aldehyde can be derived by the dehydrogenation of the corresponding alcohol."

He slowly wrote the equation representing the conversion of methyl alcohol to formaldehyde and followed that with a similar equation relating ethyl alcohol and acetaldehyde. He went on to describe the necessary conditions. This would lead easily, later on, into a discussion of the partially ionic character of the carbonyl group and of its resonance forms.

But why should anyone want to kill Ralph? If Professor Ranke was displeased with him, he could order him out of his research group, as he had, and surely that was revenge enough to state his anger. If Professor Foster was displeased with him, a bold C stamped eternally upon the student's record was, again, surely revenge enough.

And if they had motive, even if they had motive, how could they apply this particular method of murder. They didn't know enough about what went on in the boy's research. But Brade knew.

And Brade had the beginning of a motive.

He could avoid thinking of it no further. He could see Jean Makris's long face again, feel the warmth of her breath on his chin as she had exploded with "He *hated* you."

And *she* had hated Ralph. The hate had oozed out of

her and had lifted the hair on Brade's arms with its intensity.

But why should she have hated Ralph? There are a number of reasons, of course, for one person to hate another or, particularly, for a girl to hate a boy. But which reason was it in this case? And, damn it, why should Ralph have hated Brade? What reason had Brade ever given him for hate?

He had *helped* the boy, come to his side when others had deserted him. For a moment, Brade felt the not unpleasant pang of self-pity.

"The ease with which aldehydes are oxidized means, of course, that they are excellent reducing agents. This fact is of use both in the characterization of aldehydes and in organic synthesis, generally. It is also of first importance in sugar analysis. Formerly, one application of the last was in the detection of sugar in the urine with the consequent diagnosis of diabetes but that application has been replaced by an enzymatic method."

But whatever the reason, Ralph's hatred was dangerous. If the police found that hate, they would grub beneath it to find its foundation and that foundation might contain something that could be construed into a motive on Brade's part. The recipient of hate might have reason to kill the hater. And if both opportunity and motive pointed to Brade, he was backed into a corner indeed.

The girl might have been lying. But then, why should she lie?

"In addition to formalin, which as I have said, is merely a solution of formaldehyde in water (and with which those of you who are taking a premedical course may become familiar when you study anatomy next year) there is another way in which formaldehyde can be easily handled. That is in the form of paraformaldehyde, a polymer produced by the action of—"

His voice remained level throughout.

It was easier for him to do this, perhaps, because of the hidden duel he was conducting with the students. They were watching him, waiting for his voice to crack, for his wits to wander, for him to show by some sign how profoundly he had been affected by yesterday's events. Without that, they would feel cheated, and Brade felt bound to cheat them.

The bell sounded at last and Brade put down his chalk. "We will consider the various addition products of the carbonyl compounds on Monday," he said, and walked toward the door.

He did not, this time, wait for the inevitable handful of students to come up with their questions. There was another problem for the social scientists; it was virtually the same group of students who came up each time. Some, no doubt, thought they were currying favor. Some might just enjoy feeling conspicuous. Some might be trying to annoy by asking questions designed to show the lecturer's errors or ignorance. And a few (and it was for these that Brade endured the others patiently) might thirst genuinely for either explanation or further knowledge.

This time, he abandoned them all and left—his only concession to the tension of the day.

He found Cap Anson in his office waiting for him, looking through a new book on heterocyclic chemistry (it was volume one of what promised to be a ten volume project) that Brade had received three days earlier.

Anson looked up as Brade opened the door (there was

once a time when this room had been Anson's office) and his old face wrinkled into a smile.

"Ah, Brade! Good!" Anson sat down at one of the long ends of the conference table in Brade's office. (It would seat ten and was used sometimes for informal seminars among Brade's graduate students.) Anson spread out a sheaf of manuscript and looked expectant. "Have you read the revision of Chapter 5?"

Brade almost laughed with relief. It *was* relief. It was like a spring inside himself unwinding with a little pop. Students might die and policemen might question and every person he met might approach him with reaction to death in his eyes, but Anson, good old predictable Cap Anson, would think only of his book.

Brade said, "I'm sorry, Cap. I didn't get around to it."

The shadow of disappointment lay suddenly heavy upon the small man. (He was a small man only physically, of course, a careful dresser still, tightly and whitely collared, his jacket carefully buttoned about his spare figure. In recent years, he had taken to carrying a cane but if ever he touched it to the ground it could only have been when no one was looking.)

He said, "I thought last night—"

"I know I promised to discuss the Berzelius matter with you and to read the revision. I'm sorry I had to break that appointment." Brade felt like adding, defensively, that it was the first time he had ever done so, but he refrained.

"Well, never mind that, but surely after you returned home you had a chance to look at the manuscript." His blue eyes (still sharp, still intensely alive) pleaded with him, as though Brade might, if he only tried, recall that he had read the chapter after all.

"I was a little upset last night, Cap. I'm sorry. I'll read

it with you now, if you wish, and see what I can pick up as I go along."

"No." With hands slightly shaking, Cap Anson gathered his papers together. "I want you to give it thought. It's an important chapter. I'm approaching organic chemistry as a modern systematic science in this chapter and the transition is a delicate one. I'll visit your place tomorrow morning."

"Well, now, it will be Saturday, and if it's mild, I've promised Doris I'd take my daughter to the zoo."

That seemed to remind Anson of something. He said, sharply, "Your girl did give you the copy of the manuscript I gave her, didn't she?"

"Oh, yes."

"Ah. Well, I'll see you tomorrow morning."

He rose. He made no reference to Brade's statement that he was planning an outing with his daughter. It wasn't his way to do so and Brade had not expected him to. Anson had a book to do and he was not concerned with other matters.

The book! It was as though out of his own trouble, Brade had found a new depth of pity and he pitied Cap Anson intensely. Anson had been successful, great, honored—and he had lived too long.

His really great days, when he ruled organic chemistry with an inflexible rod, when his adverse comment could ruin a budding hypothesis, when the papers he presented at convention were attended by awed crowds, were two decades in the past.

When Brade took his doctorate under the man, Anson was already a veteran, an elder statesman, and organic chemistry was beginning to pass him by.

A new day had dawned. The chemistry lab had gone

electronic. Brade confessed to himself guiltily that he too fought it, but it was true. Chemistry had become instrumentation and mathematics, reaction mechanisms and kinetics. The old-fashioned chemistry that had been an art and a feeling was gone.

Anson was left with his art only and chemists spoke of him as a great man who had died. Except that, unaccountably, a small body, resembling Anson in his later days, still occasionally wandered about the hotel corridors at chemical conventions.

And so, as professor emeritus, Anson turned to his great retirement project—a definitive history of organic chemistry, a recounting of the days when giants had molded air, water and coal into substances unparalleled in nature.

But, thought Brade suddenly, was this anything more than escape? Wasn't it a colossal turning away from reality; the reality of what the physical chemists were doing to Anson's beloved reactions and a return to the older day in which Anson had been supreme.

Cap Anson was at the door before Brade remembered and said, "Oh, by the way, Cap—"

Anson turned, "Yes."

"I am going to be giving a series of lectures on lab safety starting next week and I would appreciate it if you would have the time to give one or two of the lectures yourself. After all, Cap, there's nobody here with the lab experience you've had."

Anson frowned. "Laboratory safety? Oh, yes—your boy, Neufeld. He died."

Brade thought: Then he *does* know.

Brade said, "That was one of the reasons we decided to give the lectures. Yes."

But Anson's face had suddenly contorted into sheer fury, and he brought his cane up high and then plunged it down upon the table so that it resounded like a pistol crack. "Your student died, and you did it, Brade. You did it!"

6

BRADE was frozen in his place, partly by the sharp shock of the cane-crack, much more so by the horrible force of Anson's words. His hand fumbled backward for the arm of his chair as though it had a blind passion of its own to guide the body to which it belonged into a sitting position. It touched only air.

Anson said, more quietly, "You can't deny responsibility, Brade."

Brade said, "Cap, I—I—"

"You were his research instructor. His every action in the laboratory was your responsibility. You should have known the kind of man he was. You should have known his every deed, every thought. You should have pounded him into sense or kicked him out, as Ranke did."

"You mean *moral* responsibility." Brade felt weak and glad as though moral responsibility for the death of a young man were nothing. He found the chair and sat down. "Now, Cap, there's a limit to the care a professor can take of his students."

"You haven't reached it. And I'm not blaming only you. It's all part of the general attitude today. Research has become a game. A Ph.D. is a consolation prize awarded for inhabiting a laboratory for a couple of years while the professor spends his time in his office composing applications for grants.

"In my day, a Ph.D. was *earned*. A student wasn't paid for it. There's nothing that cheapens a genuine achievement as much as to do it for money. My students worked themselves to death for a doctorate and starved for it and a few of them didn't get it even so. But those that succeeded have something they knew couldn't be bought or finagled. It had to be bled for. And it was worth it to them. You read the papers we turned out. You read them."

Brade said, with genuine respect, "You know I've read them, Cap. Most of them are classics."

"Huh." Anson allowed himself to be somewhat mollified. "How do you suppose they became classics. Because I *drove* them. I was in on Sundays, when I had to be, and by God, so were they. I worked through the night if I had to and so, by God, did they.

"I checked them constantly. I knew their every thought. Each one of my students brought in his duplicate sheets once a week and went over it with me page by page and word by word. Now tell me what you know about Neufeld's duplicate sheets."

Brade muttered, "Not as much as I should." He felt uncomfortably warm. Cap Anson was extreme, but much of what he said was true enough to hurt. It had been Anson who had introduced the duplicate notebook into the university, consisting of double sheets throughout, white and yellow.

All research data; all details of all experiments (all thoughts, ideally) were recorded and the yellow duplicate sheets, as carbons, were torn out along perforated lines and given at intervals to the research professor.

Brade carried on the custom, as did most of the department now, but not quite in the same spirit that Anson had.

Anson, after all, was a man of legend. They told stories about him. Some were the same stories that were told about every other eccentric professor in history. And yet there were stories that might well be true and illustrated his capacity for infinite detail.

There was the story of how he came to the lab one Christmas Day, the only living individual within the empty chemistry building (he needed a master key to enter) and spent the day painstakingly examining the laboratories of his students to the last desk and beaker. The next day he presented his astonished and discomfited youngsters (they knew better than to be absent the day *after* Christmas) with a list of chemicals out of alphabetical arrangement, a pinpointed roster of stock solution bottles without an upended beaker over the tip, a rollcall of departures from Anson's own absolute standards of safety and cleanliness.

All this, with his own sarcastic and highly personal remarks added.

One of the students purloined the list and as each one of those mentioned on it finally obtained his doctorate, those comments applying to him were read at the celebration dinner hosted (invariably) by Anson himself. Even Anson smiled grimly and added a few more caustic remarks from memory.

And his students had always idolized him; Brade, too, in his days as Anson's student.

Now, in the mellowness of years, there was little of the old Anson left; just an old man whom everyone dealt with gently for the sake of what had been.

Brade said, "Cap, did you know Ralph?"

"Eh? No. I passed him in the hall a number of times. To me he was just another one of these physical chemists rattling about in an organic laboratory."

"Did you know anything about his work?"

"I know it involved kinetics. That's all."

Brade was disappointed. It had suddenly occurred to him that Anson still talked to students, still inquired about their work, still offered advice. He might have talked to Ralph; he might have known more about the boy than Brade himself did. But apparently the boy's unfriendliness had been absolute. Cap Anson had not managed to penetrate it, either.

But all this talk had brought back a faint whiff of the old days, when it was Cap, after all, to whom you went with your troubles. Brade said, "I've been told a funny thing, Cap. It's been bothering me all morning. I've been told that Ralph Neufeld hated me."

Cap Anson sat down again, put his slightly arthritic left leg straight out under the table and carefully laid his cane along the table top. He said, calmly, "Quite likely."

"That he hated me? Why?"

"It's easy to hate your research professor. He's got his degree. You haven't. He assigns the problems. You work at them. You perform your experiments. He shrugs and suggests new ones. You have theories. He punches holes in them. A research professor, if he's any good, is the plague of his student's lives. A student, if he has any spirit, hates his professor until he finds out later on how much good the plaguing has done him." Anson sighed reminiscently. "Do you suppose my students loved me?"

"I should think they would have."

"Well, they didn't. Looking back on it, they may think now they did, but they didn't then. It wasn't love I wanted; it was work. And I got it. You don't remember Kinsky; he was before your time."

"I know *of* Kinsky," said Brade, gently. "I've heard him speak."

He certainly knew of Kinsky. Of all Anson's students, Joseph Kinsky had turned out best. He was part of the Wisconsin group now and permanently famous for his tetracycline syntheses and the new light on antibiotic action that had come about as an indirect result.

Anson grinned. "He was the best. Absolutely the best of my boys."

(He loved to talk about Kinsky. Brade well remembered a faculty dinner after which the brash Foster had said, "Hey, Cap, doesn't it gripe you to have Kinsky a bigger man than you ever were?"

(Foster, ordinarily not a drinker, must have had a few cocktails inside himself or he would not have said it so baldly or stood there grinning so fatuously. Brade had winced and shot a hostile glance at the moist-lipped Foster. It was an obvious attempt to hurt the old man.

(The old man was a match for Foster, however. Shorter by half a head, he gave a towering impression. He said, "Foster, there are two times when jealousy is not likely to exist. A father is not jealous of his son. A teacher is not jealous of his pupil. If the men I train are better than I, it may be because they had the better teacher. All their accomplishments reflect creditably upon me. What I do as a chemist gives mankind the achievements of one man. What I do as a teacher gives mankind the achievements of many. My bitter regret is not that Kinsky outshines me, but that every student I've ever had does not outshine me equally."

(He had not raised his voice, but conversation in the room had stopped with Foster's remark, and Anson's answer had rung out clearly. There was actually a subdued patter of applause and to Brade's own delight, Foster had looked as though two donkey's ears attached to his skull would have completed an ensemble that lacked only that.)

Was Anson thinking of that, too? Brade thought: probably not.

Anson was saying, "Do you suppose Kinsky didn't hate me? There were times when he could have killed me. We were at daggers' points almost constantly. For God's sake, Brade, I could wish *you* had hated me a little more."

"I never hated you at all, Cap."

"That's because I was getting soft and that's probably why my boys weakened too. I had had hopes for you, Brade."

Brade felt pain at the wording. Anson "had had" hopes. He had them no longer. He would never speak of Brade as he spoke of Kinsky. Well, he thought savagely, was he surprised? What did he expect?

Anson said suddenly, "By the way, Kinsky will be visiting us. Have I told you that?"

"No."

"I received a letter from him yesterday but, then, I didn't see you yesterday, did I?" Anson produced the letter and glared at Brade.

Brade smiled self-consciously and took the letter. It

was short. It simply gave routine greetings, stated that Kinsky was in town on business and hoped to be at the university the next Monday at which time he would be delighted to talk over Anson's book though he, Kinsky, felt certain he could add very little to Anson's experience and knowledge. And it ended with routine goodbyes.

Brade said, "This coming Monday."

"That's right. And I'll want you to meet him. Fellow students, you know." Anson got heavily to his feet, put away the letter and took his cane in his hand. "I'll see you tomorrow morning, Brade."

"All right, Cap, but don't forget about those safety lectures now."

Left alone, Brade felt a renewed heaviness of mind. Cap Anson might talk of student hatred as though it were an accolade, a sign of the excellence of the teacher, but none of his argument applied to Brade. Brade had not driven Ralph; he had saved him, rather, from the consequences of Ranke's rejection. He had helped Ralph; he had been as easy with him as he could, ignored his peculiarities and allowed him to find his own way.

Why should Ralph have hated him?

Or was Jean Makris lying?

But then why should she lie?

Could she have been mistaken?

How could she be corroborated? Who would know the queer, untouchable Ralph well enough to do the corroborating—or the contradicting?

Brade didn't know, but, damn it, there were those who were close to him, unavoidably close to him through the exigencies of work. His other research students. Ralph's brothers-in-science.

He looked at the clock on the wall. It was not quite

eleven. There was nothing important that needed doing before lunch. Nothing important compared to this, certainly.

He walked down the hall and looked into Charles Emmett's laboratory. He was there, though Roberta wasn't. He said, quietly, "Charlie, could I speak to you for a few moments?"

Emmett put down his separatory funnel and the two liquids it contained settled out and separated in a swirl of bubbles. He lifted the funnel's glass stopper a moment to let the vapors puff off, then replaced it.

"Sure, Professor Brade," he said.

Brade sat on the swivel chair at his desk while Emmett pulled over one of the straight chairs that stood about the conference table.

He said, "It was a tough break for Ralph, sir."

"Yes, it was. A tough break for the department, too; for us; for me. It's what I want to talk about in a way."

Did Emmett look apprehensive at that? Brade tried not to watch him too narrowly. Of his four students (three now), Emmett had been with him the longest and was, in a way, the least promising. He was a hard plugger, hard enough to suit even Cap Anson; but no one would ever accuse him of any sign of brilliance.

He sat there now, somewhat bulky, with ruddy hair and freckled arms to the ends of which were attached large hands. He wore clear-rimmed glasses a trifle small for his face.

Brade liked him for his equanimity. Sometimes he thought he could do without brilliance if only a student could withstand an experiment that failed and not plummet into despair. When an experiment failed Emmett, he simply ran another designed a little differently. He might not see the ingenious thing to do, but presumably he would get somewhere eventually. And in any case, in comparison with the emotional unevenness of the average high-tension student, Emmett's quiet was as warming as soup to Brade and as comforting as bread.

Brade said, "Now that this terrible thing has happened to Ralph, I find I feel a certain guilt. I feel ashamed at—at not having known him better. I might have helped him more. And of course, this holds for my other students. For you. I should know you better."

Emmett squirmed a bit. "Hell, Professor Brade, I have no complaints. We get along."

"I'm glad to hear you say so. But it bothers me anyway. For instance, we haven't talked about your research in almost a month. Has anything gone wrong?"

"No, sir. I'm all set for the coming spring. The historical section of my dissertation is done, and I have the preliminary data down cold. I just need a few more derivatives."

Brade nodded. Emmett's problem dealt with the synthesis of certain thiazolidones which had not, hitherto, been prepared by the usual methods of ring closure. A problem like that had its advantages and disadvantages.

In such a synthesis, a student needed no esoteric mathematics or breath-holding quantitation. He need only patience and a little bit of luck.

On the other hand, he did need that little bit of luck. Sometimes a synthesis could not be carried through by any method student and professor happened to hit upon. Or a synthesis might be worked out and then anticipated by other workers. In either case, the Ph.D. was quashed and a new problem had to be assigned.

Brade said, as lightly as he could, "Then before long you'll be passing out of the hate stage."

Emmett looked honestly blank. "What?"

"Cap Anson was just telling me a Ph.D. student invariably hates his professor."

"Hell, he's kidding. That's just old Cap talking. Some of the boys pop off about their profs sometimes but nothing much."

Brade was conscious now (as he had not been previously under similar circumstances) of Emmett's informality of address. Ranke's students always gave the impression of standing at attention when they spoke to *him*. (Well, thought Brade, is that what I want? A salute? A heel-click?).

He said, "What about Ralph?"

A veil fell over Emmett's eyes. "Beg pardon?"

"What about Ralph, Charlie? What was his attitude toward me?"

"Well." Emmett cleared his throat elaborately. "I didn't know him very well. Hardly anyone did. He didn't talk much."

"But he didn't like me, did he?"

Emmett considered that for a moment. "He didn't like anyone. Well, anyway—" He made to stand up.

Brade put out his hand. "Wait. You're not answering my question. It's a little late to be interested in him, but I am. I want to know—He didn't like me, did he?"

It was dragged out of Emmett with hooks. "Well, no, professor, I suppose he didn't."

"Why didn't he? Do you know?" (There was something undignified about this questioning of one student about another. Brade was painfully aware of this. But he had to know.)

"As near as I can make out, sir, it was because he was a dumb jerk." Emmett looked suddenly stricken. "I didn't mean to say that."

Brade said, edgily, "Oh, let's not be superstitious about speaking ill of the dead. If there's good to be said, it's when people are alive and can appreciate a word of praise that they should have it. It does a corpse no good. There's too much of this praise-him-when-he's-dead-but-not-a-second-before attitude."

"Well, he joined us once when we were bull-sessioning around, hanging at the edge of the group. We were talking about the faculty. You know."

"I know," said Brade, with a sudden clear recollection of his own student days.

"And someone said Foster was getting to be a kind of Simon Legree, you know, or something like that, and Neufeld butted in and said the other kind were worse; the kind that let a student sink or swim and never gave a damn. Like you, sir, he said."

Brade nodded. "I see." Had he drawn hate for the reverse of Cap Anson's reasoning? Had Ralph resented too great freedom?

Emmett said, "But I tell you what, sir. I don't think it was hate, exactly. I'd sometimes watch him during seminars when you were talking; the way he'd look at you; especially the last few months. It's a funny thing." He lapsed into silence.

"Well," said Brade, rasped to a fine edge. "*Well?*"

"I'm no psychologist, Professor Brade. But still in all, I don't think he hated you, the way he acted. It seems to me he was scared of you. Scared *stiff!*"

7

"AFRAID of me?" said Brade, with energy. (Good God, this was worse than the other.) "Afraid of *what*, Charlie?"

"There you've got me, I don't know, professor."

They stared at one another.

Then Brade said, "Are you sure, Charlie? I'm quite upset about all this and I feel I must know: Is there any reason at all to explain his being afraid of me?"

Brade was beginning to feel a helplessness in the face of Ralph's death, of everything concerning it, of everything it touched. It was something impossible unless he himself were the murderer. Was it also something motiveless unless he himself had a motive? *What* motive?

Emmett turned a dull red. "I don't like to say this— But if you must know and keep it confidential about where you heard it—"

"*Say* it."

"I don't know anything, you see. But I know who would, if anyone would."

"Oh? Who?"

"Roberta, sir."

"Roberta Goodhue?" said Brade, blankly, though he

knew no other Roberta than this other Ph.D. student of his.

"That's right. I couldn't help but—I mean, it's a secret, I suppose, but being Roberta is my labmate, sometimes I can't help but notice things or hear things." His embarrassment had reached the acutely painful stage. "Well, she was kind of close to him."

"How do you mean, close?" An uncomfortable suspicion swept over Brade. Lord, he knew *nothing* about his students.

"Don't get me wrong, Professor Brade. All I'm saying is they went out together; had a couple of dates. I don't know if it went any further and I haven't anything to say about that. A couple of dates; that's all I know about. But even a couple of dates means something. I mean a fellow is likely to talk more about himself to a girl over a dinner table than to a bunch of guys in a lunchroom. See what I mean?"

"Yes, of course." Brade nodded, thoughtfully. "Is Roberta in today?"

"I haven't seen her, professor."

"I suppose she knows what happened."

"I think so. I heard that Jean Makris called her." A queer half-smile played over his lips for an instant and left before Brade could be sure it was there.

"Well, thank you, Charlie. Thanks for helping out. That's about all."

"Okay. And you won't say anything to Roberta, sir? I mean, about where you heard it."

"I'll be careful."

He rose to open the door for Emmett and caught sight of another boy skulking (it was the word that occurred to him) in the corridor outside. It took a second look for him to pin down the second youngster to an identity, and then it was only Gregory Simpson, his newest student, the one who had shared Ralph's laboratory.

"You want to see me, Greg?" he asked.

"If you have a few minutes, Professor Brade," said Simpson. He had a tenor voice, light eyebrows that were almost invisible so that his pale eyes had a naked appearance. His round nose gave his face a comical but good-natured shape.

"Surely. Come in."

The two students barely nodded to one another and Simpson slid through the door.

Simpson was an earnest young man, but somehow not very impressive. (Brade sighed. The impressive young men followed the grants.)

He said, "Well, Greg, what's up?"

Simpson took the seat Emmett had just vacated. He said, uneasily, "I was thinking about where to stay?"

"Where to stay? Aren't you at one of the dormitories?"

"No, I mean here, Professor Brade. In the laboratories."

"Oh." Brade felt at a loss. "But what's your problem?"

"Well, the lab. Ralph Neufeld died—I mean—"

"You mean you think you can't use it any more."

"Well—"

Brade said sharply, "This thing is finished, you know. Done. The lab is yours, all yours till a new student is assigned to share it with you."

Simpson sat silent for a moment but did not look as though his problem were solved. He made no move to leave.

Brade said, "Doesn't that settle things, Greg?"

"Not exactly, professor. I would rather have another lab, if it's possible."

"Do you think this one is, uh—jinxed?"

"No-o."

"Are you afraid Ralph's ghost will come back and haunt you?" Brade tried to keep that from sounding too contemptuously sarcastic, but he was having a hard day and his store of patience was running dry.

Simpson rubbed at his invisible eyebrows. "Nothing like that. I just—I just thought if it were possible to change—If it isn't, I guess that's all right." He looked completely miserable.

Brade repented his sharpness. A man, after all, wasn't entirely responsible for irrational fears instilled by an irrational society, and who could say he was free of them.

He said, "All right, Greg, I understand. Look, I tell you what. You won't be starting research till the end of the semester anyway, so why don't you make your headquarters in Emmett's lab. All you'll be doing there is to read occasionally, and Charlie will give you drawer space. By next semester, when you actually dive into experimental work, Charlie will be just working on his thesis and you can take his place. I'll put a new man in your present lab when the time comes."

Simpson lit up as though someone had pulled an internal switch. "Hey, thanks, Professor Brade. That's swell. Thanks."

Brade smiled tightly at him and then said, "But wait!"

Simpson, who had arisen, sat down again and clouded.

It occurred to Brade, quite suddenly, that Ralph was not the only one with access to his laboratory among the students. Simpson, as second man in the laboratory, had a key of his own.

Brade said, "This is another subject altogether, Greg, and confidential, completely confidential. There have been cases of petty thievery in the building."

"Oh?" The student's voice dropped automatically to a conspiratorial whisper.

"We're investigating a bit and I wonder if at any time in the last month you had reason to think some unauthorized person was inside your laboratory."

Simpson bowed his head and thought. Then he said, his pale eyes lifting to meet Brade's with wide candor in them, "No, sir."

"Nothing at all suspicious? Something out of place unexpectedly? Something missing you thought should have been there?"

"No, sir. Nothing at all."

"Perhaps Ralph may have mentioned something of the sort?"

"Oh, no, Professor Brade." The youngster said it quickly and with emphasis.

"Are you sure?"

"Positive. Ralph never said a word to me. Not one at any time. I tried saying 'Hello' to him when I would come into lab but he never answered, so I quit. He gave me the impression that he resented having me there; you know, as though it were his lab and I had no right coming in. Once I just came *near* his desk when he was writing up an experiment; at least, I think that was what he was doing; and he closed his notebook and whirled on me as though he were ready to kill me. I never came within six feet of him again. Not that I mean to say he wasn't a nice guy."

"I understand. Now that he's dead."

"Pardon?"

"You must have resented this attitude of his."

Simpson said cautiously, "I just ignored him. I'd been warned about him, actually."

"Warned about what?"

"The way he picked fights. Things like that."

"Did you get into a fight with him?"

"I just stayed away from him. We had no trouble."

Brade said, "You're twenty-two, aren't you?"

Simpson looked astonished. "Yes, sir."

Brade nodded. "Well, all right, Greg. Now your problem is settled. Right?"

"Yes, Professor Brade. Thanks a lot. Thanks."

Brade sat alone in his office now and considered what to do next. Simpson, he felt reasonably certain, was out. He was a young, harmless boy. From all Brade had managed to observe about him, he was mild-tempered and passive, the kind who would avoid a quarrel by retreat exactly as he himself had described.

Of course, the kind who avoided an open break lost the opportunity to blow off steam. The pressure could build up within and eventually seek an outlet through some subterranean course of revenge—

Hell, how was he going to straighten this thing out? He was no detective. He didn't know, really, what to do next.

He picked up the telephone and dialed his home. Doris answered, her "Hello" neutral. It gave no indication as to the state of her feelings.

"Hello, Doris. Everything all right?"

"Of course. What about you, though? What did Littleby want?"

He told her in a few words. She listened without interrupting, then said, "How did he sound?"

"Well, not exactly pleased."

"Did he imply it was your fault?"

"No. But there was a kind of guilt-by-association attitude about him. It's bad publicity for the school, and it's my student and that tars me. It's my opinion he'd rather we didn't show up at his place tomorrow night."

"Well, it's my opinion we'll be there," said Doris, flatly.

"I realize that. I said we were coming."

A short pause, then Doris said, "How do you feel?"

"Peculiar. I'm a kind of celebrity. You should have seen my class. I don't think one of them heard a word I said. All waiting for me to collapse, or pull a gun and start shooting or something. Cap Anson was a real relief."

"Oh? What did he do?"

"Nothing. That's where the relief lay. He was waiting for me after class and started talking about his book. It was the only touch of normality about today." He decided to say nothing about Anson's calm assumption of an appointment for the next morning. Not on the phone.

Doris said, "All right. Take care of yourself and listen, Lou, don't play detective. Do you know what I mean?"

"I know what you mean. Good-bye, Doris."

He smiled grimly at the closed connection. Don't play detective? Good Lord, if he only knew how to play it adequately.

He picked up the telephone again, pushing the button that connected him with the office switchboard and asked for Jean Makris.

"Miss Makris? Professor Brade."

"Yes, Professor Brade. Is there something I can do for you?"

"Can you get me Roberta Goodhue's home phone

number?" He had it himself somewhere but he was in no mood to begin filing through a miscellany of cards.

Jean Makris's voice took on a livelier tone. "Sure, Professor. Isn't she in today?"

"I think not."

"Well, I *hope* she's not sick." But her voice sounded quite cheerful. "Do you want me to make the call for you?"

"No, just give me the number, if you please. And Miss Makris?"

"Yes, Professor Brade?"

"Did you call Roberta to tell her about the accident up here?"

"Well, yes. Shouldn't I have? I thought she ought to know, being as she was a fellow student and, well—"

"I see. Did you call Mr. Emmett and Mr. Simpson, the other fellow students?"

This time there was a pause and the secretary's voice when it came again seemed uncomfortable. "Well, no, Professor Brade, I didn't. You see—"

But Brade cut her off. "I see. Never mind. Give me Roberta's number."

He dialed the number and the phone rang a number of times before the receiver was lifted. "Yes?" The voice was subdued.

"Roberta? This is Professor Brade."

"Oh. Hello, Professor Brade. Don't tell me there was a seminar this morning and I'd forgotten about it."

"No, nothing like that, Roberta. I called to ask how you are?"

"Oh." There was a pause and Brade imagined she was gathering her strength to sound reasonably normal. "I'm all right. I'll be in for the lab."

"Are you sure you can make it."

"Quite sure."

"Well, then, Roberta, if you're well, I wonder—" (He paused to look at the clock. It was at twenty of twelve and he felt uncomfortable about rushing her but, hell, she lived just off campus and could walk over in five minutes) "I wonder if you can come in as early as twelve?"

Another pause. "If you'll give me fifteen minutes, I'll be there."

"Good. And what do you say, let's have lunch together."

Again a pause. Then, guardedly, "Is there something you want to discuss with me, Professor Brade?"

Brade saw no point in trying to be evasive. He said, "Yes."

She said, "About my research?"

He said, "No. Personal matters."

"I'll be there, Professor."

"Good." He hung up.

Brade looked over the afternoon schedule. The laboratory sessions would deal with aldehydes and ketones, of course. The preparation of a silver mirror, one of those useless but spectacular experiments that kept student interest alive, was on tap. Also, the preparation of a sulfite addition product, which presented no difficulties, except for the washing of the precipitate. That involved the use of either which was, of course, highly flammable. However, no open flames were called for in today's experiments and any student who tried to smoke had been well warned that expulsion from the course was the penalty for the first offense against the more fundamental safety rules.

Still, on this day, damn it, accidents must be ruled out. He would make a point of this to Charlie Emmett.

Brade wished earnestly he could skip lab this once. There was no absolute commitment on his part to be there, but as a rule he made it a point to show up for at least a short time. In the first place, there might be questions the lab assistants could not answer, and in the second his appearance was good for student morale. It always made a laboratory course seem somewhat cheap and unimportant if the lecturing professor ostentatiously did not attend.

And yet, Charlie Emmett was certainly capable of running the laboratory by himself. This was his second year and with Roberta helping at the reagent counter, there should be no trouble.

Well, wait and see.

Roberta Goodhue knocked softly on Professor Brade's office door and Brade reached for his hat and coat as she came in.

He smiled and said, rather stiffly, "Would you object to going to the Riverside Inn? We'll take my car and I'll have you back by one."

"It's all right." She seemed not very interested. She was a short girl, her slight dumpiness accentuated by the cut of the salmon-pink cloth coat she was wearing. She was dark in complexion and probably unhappy (Brade thought) over her hirsuteness. He did not recall noticing it before, but she had a faint mustache and a line of sparse hairs down the cheek.

She wasn't exactly ugly; but she was certainly not pretty. He said, "Why don't you meet me at the main door? I just want to drop in to Charlie's and tell him to check on open flames today."

The Riverside Inn was well-filled, but they had an al-
cove to themselves with a view of the river and of the
highway that lined it. (Nature unalloyed was becoming a
rarer commodity each year.)

He said, "I imagine you are distressed over what happened yesterday."

They had given their orders and Roberta sat there,
crumbling her roll and staring at the four lanes of
speeding automobiles. She said, in a whisper, "Yes."

"I have—an idea" (he didn't know how to put it)
"that you were—friendly with Ralph."

Roberta looked up at him and suddenly her eyes were
wet and brimming with tears. "We were to have been
married as soon as he got his degree."

8

THE waitress came and distributed a breaded veal chop
for Brade, and egg salad for Roberta, cups of coffee and
little containers of cream for both. That introduced a wel-
come interruption during which Brade had time to catch
his breath.

He said, "I'm terribly sorry. I had no idea the situation
was like that. You should not have come in—I didn't
know."

"It's all right. It's better, I suppose. It would be worse if I stayed home." She seemed to collect herself, gather scraps of energy so she could look at him firmly. "Is it Ralph you want to talk about?"

Brade groped for something to say. "I don't want to sound ghoulish but there is the question of what to do about his research. However, under these circumstances—"

She was frowning. "Are you going to continue the work he's done?"

"Well, no need to discuss the matter now. Another time." This had been foolish, he thought drearily, dragging a girl off to quiz her about a fiance dead less than a day. But how was he to have known!

Roberta was watching him intently. She said, "I suppose you didn't like him."

Brade finished. Had she read that in his troubled look? He said, "No, that's not right. I thought highly of him."

"Thank you for saying that, but I expect you didn't. I know that very few people liked him, and I can understand why." She was crumbling her roll again and had abandoned her salad after one mouthful. "He was a peculiar person, very much on the defensive. It took time to get past the prickliness, but when you did, you found he was very nice. Sensitive. Affectionate." She paused. "I was with his mother most of last night. Poor woman. Oh, *how* could it have happened? I can't *believe* he could have made such a foolish mistake."

Brade said quickly, "Did he have any relatives besides his mother?"

"No." She looked at him for a moment. "You don't know anything about Ralph, do you, Professor Brade? I mean about his private life?"

"I'm afraid not, Roberta. I feel now I should be closer to my students, take a greater personal interest. But this can't be a pleasant conversation for you."

"Talking about him is all I have left," said Roberta. She looked intently down on her plate and a few strands of her straight hair, somewhat sketchily tied into a tail behind, fell over her forehead. "He wasn't American-born, you know."

"Oh?" (Brade had known that much.)

"His mother and he were the only survivors of—something unpleasant. He never told me the details but we don't really need them, do we? His father was shot to death and he had had an older sister who was killed—somehow.

"He was afraid of the world. Life wasn't easy in America either, you know. A strange land, a strange language. I suppose he was too afraid even to really trust anyone, ever to feel comfortable about another's good intentions. It got to be a fixed habit. Do you know what I mean?"

"I think I understand, Roberta."

"And it was a vicious circle. Because he couldn't relax and accept people, they grew hard to him and were cruel. And then he was forced to do foolish things. It was hard for him to work with another student; he always felt that things would be taken from him; the way his family was; the way his childhood was. When it seemed to him another student was taking one of the beakers he himself had washed, he went wild and attacked. It wasn't a rational action but you can see how he wouldn't be rational when things like that happened. But did Professor Ranke try to understand? He kicked him out. To Ralph, it was just another rejection. It made him more withdrawn than ever."

"So that he hated me, too, didn't he, Roberta?"

She stiffened. Her voice grew sharp. "Who told you that?"

"I'm just guessing."

"Jean Makris told you, didn't she?"

Brade said, uncomfortably, "Why do you say that?"

Roberta's nostrils flared and her mouth was pinched. Then she drew a deep breath. "It doesn't matter anymore. You might as well know. Ralph went out with her once or twice before—before we got friendly. It was nothing, just something casual, but the stupid girl took it more seriously than it was worth.

"She kept after him and after him when it was all over between them. She was *vindictive* about it. She called me yesterday evening. She was *happy* he was dead; and happy she could tell *me* about it." She spoke with a controlled violence.

Brade stirred restlessly. If the death of Ralph did one thing, it was to rile the mud at the bottom of the pure academic stream and make it resemble pretty much the other portions of the murky river of life.

He said, "Then you don't think Ralph had cause to hate me?"

"No cause. I never heard him say he hated you. Of course, just at first—"

"Yes?"

"He was very uncertain about his research. Professor Ranke had kicked him out, and he felt a failure. It made him feel inadequate and uncertain so that perhaps he might have expressed worries about you to Jean Makris when they were out. He must have, I suppose, because once when she called him—after he wasn't seeing her, anymore—she implied that she could make trouble if she told you how he really felt about you. Ralph told me about that. He was very bitter. Only she waited until he was dead and then—couldn't even let his dead body rest in peace."

She gulped and started to cry softly.

Brade pushed what was left of his chop to one side, drank his coffee, and signaled for the check.

"You'd better have your coffee," he urged, "and don't feel bad about his relations with me. We got along well and even if he had disliked me, I think you have explained why that would be and I understand." He had a strong urge to reach out and pat her hand but resisted.

She did sip at her coffee and the waitress came with the check.

In the car, driving back uptown, Brade said, "Did Ralph buy you an engagement ring, Roberta?"

She stared straight ahead, watching the road with painful concentration, but obviously seeing nothing. "No, he couldn't afford one. His mother worked to pay his tuition. She had that European attitude, you know. No sacrifice was too great to make her son a learned man. And now what has she left?"

"Had you set an actual date for the marriage?"

"It was set for when he received his degree. There was no actual date closer than that."

"Did his mother know that he was planning marriage?"

"She knew we were seeing each other. And she liked me, I think. I don't think he told her about marriage, though. I think she might not have approved. She might have felt that with his degree he could make a better match. European mothers have an exaggerated notion of the salability of a degree on the matrimonial market."

They drove through the gates onto the university grounds.

Brade did make an appearance during the laboratory period, but a very brief one. It was very quiet. Even Gerald Corwin, the accident-prone student, seemed to have avoided finding a piece of glass on which to scratch himself. In fact, he was staring at his test tube, pleased that its sides glistened metallically with aldehyde-precipitated silver making a cylindrical mirror of it. (Since he was the worst lab student in the class, it was almost a foregone conclusion that he produced the best mirror. Brade held it up for demonstration purposes for the sake of those more skillful students whose more careful manipulations had resulted in nothing but a gray-black precipitate at the bottom of the tube.)

He then spent a short time in the department office glancing over the faculty reports on Ralph Neufeld. With Jean Makris's eyes upon him, he felt uncomfortable and found himself forced to go through the cards hurriedly. He found nothing of significance in any case.

Heavy-hearted, he returned to his own office and began sketching out possible subjects for the safety lectures. There were certain subjects that had obviously to be covered. The proper use of the hood; methods of evaporation of inflammable solvents; the proper treatment of compressed-gas cylinders; water baths; wire gauzes; the bending of tubing.

Then what about the methods of using pipettes. Pipette-handling was in transition. In Brade's day, a pipette was something one stuck in the mouth to suck up a solution to carefully adjusted marks. It was an unattractive thing to do and unsafe beside, since a careless suck would place a bit of the solution right in the mouth, and the solution was corrosive or poisonous as often as not. No semester went by without at least one student surprised by a mouthful of sodium hydroxide solution.

Nowadays, the use of rubber bulbs was almost universal at the graduate level. They were used to apply suction to the pipettes and were designed with special escape valves intended to end suction at will. The difficulty was that the department hesitated to invest in the hundred or so needed to equip the undergraduate laboratory properly. Perhaps with a safety drive on, the economy motif might be softened. Brade made a note to check on that.

And then somewhere in the course of making his notes, his mind moved outward and he was left looking at midair, ball-point pen in hand.

The remarkably unlikeable Ralph had, apparently, been well liked by two young ladies; well enough to make for the rising of bitter passions. Strange!

It turned motivation in toward a new direction. It was not enough now to consider only the petty irritations of fellow students and faculty members against a young man of sharp tongue and quarrelsome disposition and to wonder how those could have been parlayed into the kind of feeling that would lead to a cold-bloodedly calculated murder.

There were now the disappointments of love to consider also. And these were feelings that led themselves more easily to killing.

Strange again! Neither girl, Jean Makris nor Roberta Goodhue, could be described as good-looking. Neither could be thought capable of inspiring love in a young man, and yet—

That was foolish! Women of all sorts got married, and

men, too. If only the Hollywood ideals of beauty were to result in passion, the race would die out quickly.

And there were virtues other than those of stylized good looks. An appearance of friendliness and sympathy might mean more to some young men than an artfully contrived system of curves. A face that carried affection in its eyes might make up for the fact that it also carried hair on its cheeks. Why not?

And a boy like Ralph, hating and fearing the world, might gravitate irresistibly to the plain girl.

How could he dare enter competition for a pretty one? How could he compete with other men and risk a new kind of rejection that might strike more deeply even than the old kinds with which he was familiar? Would he not avoid that possibility by deliberately choosing his love object in such a fashion as to be sure of acceptance? Might there not be a deliberate (if perhaps unconscious) aim at the girl who hungered more, was more apt to be grateful and pleased at attention, less apt to be pursued by competing suitors?

(Brade smiled at himself bitterly. Necessity was making him into a psychologist as well as a detective.)

And a girl like that—if she were rejected for another girl, also like that—were not hell's furies proverbially inferior?

Hope arising for her when hope was nearly gone, and then vanishing again! And it would be worse when what was lost was lost to a woman no better-looking than one's self; when one could not console one's self in the very hopelessness of the competition?

He had felt Jean Makris' hate. The question was, could that hate have been intense enough to drive her to murder? And if it had, could she have been intellectually capable of this particular crime? Would she feel sufficiently self-confident of her chemistry to risk exchanging one chemical for another? Would she know enough about Ralph's research to do so intelligently. He might have talked about it to her. She might have had a college course in chemistry. (Had she gone to college at all? He would have to find out.)

For that matter, what of Roberta herself?

The young man had abandoned one girl, he might abandon another. Roberta, abandoned, would have been as furious, presumably, as Jean Makris, abandoned, and better equipped intellectually for the murder.

Could a young man so suspicious of the world, so paranoid in nature, remain with any girl long, however loving she might have been, however sympathetic. How long would it have taken for little slights or little misunderstandings (real or fancied, it didn't matter) to build into gnawing distrust and hate in his dark and lonely heart?

Ralph hadn't given Roberta a ring. He hadn't told anyone of the engagement. Charlie Emmett hadn't known, for instance. Even his mother, apparently, hadn't been told. There was no sure objective sign that he really intended to marry Roberta. Nothing but his statement to Roberta.

She must have realized the shakiness of her position. Surely a girl was more sensitive to the nuances of the marriage proposal and its various stages of sincerity or phoniness than to anything else in the world. What if she felt he were cooling off or had never been more than lukewarm in the first place? What if she pressed him for something more definite, an actual date for the marriage, a ring, a public announcement? What if he had evaded that?

For God's sake, what if still a third plain girl appeared on the scene?

Certainly Roberta knew enough chemistry to kill him, and if she had done so, there need not be any question of acting in her attitude about it now. She had seemed desperately sincere in her sorrow, but she might still love him with one part of herself while having killed him for defection. She might still cry over her victim and be desolate.

And she would know the details of his research. She would be more likely to know than anyone else. More likely to know than even Emmett had thought. Research students always talked about their research, and if Ralph was not like the rest of them but kept to himself with pathological suspicion, surely he would make an exception in favor of his love, of the one human being that he could bring himself to trust.

But, damn it, how did he go about proving anything? Theories were fine; he could make up a dozen. Theory-making was his profession in a way. But in chemistry, he knew how to go about testing a theory. In detective work he had not a notion of such a thing as the prosaic mechanics of wresting proof from possibility.

He was going around in circles and gave up.

He looked at the clock. It was just past four.

Twenty-four hours earlier, he was thinking of going home in order to be there for his five o'clock appointment with Cap Anson. He would have picked up the manuscript, shared an aperitif with the old man, talked over an item or two, probably have invited him to dinner.

But he had stepped into Ralph's laboratory for a bit of standard acid and for the usual late-afternoon good-bye (another of the many little habits he had picked up from Cap Anson's manner of doing things in his day)—and it had all begun.

Now he was thinking of going home again, but with no pleasure and no anticipation. The manuscript of Anson's was still unread. He had not taken it out of his briefcase. His last oxygenation set-up had not even been dismantled, was just sitting there in his private lab, resinifying.

Everything was a mess.

Now a weekend was coming up. He looked about wearily for whatever he might profitably take home with him. Doris disapproved of his habit of taking papers, journals, and general miscellany (or what he called weekend trivia) home with him but, really, any faculty member who confined his work to working hours simply could not keep up.

He sighed. He was in absolutely no mood to take home anything in the nature of class work or research literature. There was Anson's manuscript in his briefcase already. He would *have* to read that tonight. Then Saturday, Anson would come, Ginny would have to be taken to the zoo, and there would be the Littleby affair in the evening. And on Sunday he might as well collapse. There would be a rough week ahead of him.

So he took nothing but the manuscript. He snapped his briefcase shut, threw his coat over his arm and took his hat.

He turned to the door and was at once startled by the misty silhouette that showed through the frosted section an instant before there was the sound of the knock.

It wasn't one of his students, nor, at first glance, one of the faculty. One got so that one could tell from the vague general outline who it might be.

He opened the door uneasily and a fat-cheeked stranger stepped in, smiling moistly and saying cheerfully, "Hello, Prof. You don't remember me?"

But Brade did at the instant of the sound of the voice. It was the plainclothesman, the one of the evening before, Jack Doheny.

9

BRADE dropped his hat and bent to pick it up. He felt his face flush, but Doheny was smiling at him blandly. The plainclothesman was chewing gum, and his jaw muscles worked rhythmically.

Brade said, "Is there anything I can do for you, Mr. Doheny? I *do* remember you, you see."

"Nope. Something I can do for *you*." Doheny reached into his inner jacket pocket and brought forth a key. "You asked me to get this for you. Thought I'd bring it over personally. It's the kid's key to his laboratory."

"Oh." A wave of relief passed over Brade. Of course. He had asked for it, and it was perfectly natural for the plainclothesman to return it. "Thank you, sir."

"Kid's only relative is a mother, you know." His eyes wandered coolly about Brade's office.

Brade, still holding his hat, stood waiting with just a

small impatience for the door to be unblocked. He said, "Yes, I know that now."

"I went over last night to break the news. It's the lousy part of my job. Found her in a bad way. She'd found out already."

"Oh, yes?"

"A girl was there with her. Another student of yours."

"Roberta Goodhue?" (She had said she had been at Ralph's mother's. She had not said anything about Doheny.)

"Yeah. She brought the news. I asked her how she'd found out. She said someone at school called her."

"The department secretary did. I had told her, and she had felt she should tell Roberta. Roberta had been— uh—friendly with the young man."

"Tough." Doheny shook his head but still made no move to step out of the way. "This your office, Prof?"

"Yes, it is."

"Very nice. Good table, this one. Could use something like it for my shop in the basement. You a do-it-your-selfer?"

"No, I'm afraid not."

"I hear professors and like that are going in for it in a big way, these days. You know, making their own furni- ture, going out camping, things like that."

Brade nodded and tried not to show his impatience.

Doheny said, "Hey, am I holding you past your time? Is this when you leave?"

"Actually my time's my own. Sometimes I stay till mid- night; sometimes I leave at noon. It depends on my lec- ture schedule and how I feel."

"Whew," said the plainclothesman with obvious sincerity, "that's the way a job ought to be. Were you staying late yesterday?"

"No, as a matter of fact, I wasn't. I was due to leave in a few minutes at the time I discovered the—the body."

"And today it looks like I'm keeping you. Well, don't mean to." He stepped out of the way, finally, without haste.

"That's all right," said Brade, stiffly. He followed Doheny out into the corridor and locked the door behind him. He put Neufeld's key on his own key ring for the present.

Doheny was watching. He said, "That's a master key you have on the ring there, right?"

Brade was annoyed. He put away the keys hastily. "I have to get into the building at all hours."

"Oh, sure. Fits all the labs?"

"It fits those that don't have special locks. I imagine most of the faculty have master keys."

"Oh, sure." Doheny smiled, nodded, chewed gum.

Brade argued with himself uselessly during the drive home. So the policeman had come again. He had had a legitimate motive. It was Brade's own request that had brought him. And his questions were perfectly normal ones; he displayed no animosity or suspicion. Why should he have?

And yet—why the questions as to when Brade had left for the night? Why the interest in the master key? How did he notice it so quickly anyway? Was he looking for it?

And why borrow trouble, eh? Brade forced his thoughts into another groove.

Dinner went off exceptionally well, considering. Ginny had heard of the incident by now. (It *had* made the newscasts, and friends had called Doris to discuss it, and Ginny had listened carefully to all her mother's phone conversations.)

She was not allowed to discuss it herself, of course, and her attempts to do so were quashed firmly by both parents. The excitement of it, however, kept her glowing through supper and caused her to eat voraciously.

That set up a beneficial feedback, since the sight of her eating without encouragement and without adverse comments on the bill of fare put Doris into a good mood which meant that she was pleasant herself and that, in turn, acted to soften some of the bands of apprehension clamping about Brade's heart.

Pleasantness carried right through dessert and the eventual (and inevitable) suggestion by Doris that Ginny transfer her scene of action upstairs where she might get her homework out of the way for the weekend, take her bath, and go to sleep.

"And I don't want to hear the television set on past nine o'clock, Virginia," said Doris.

Ginny leaned over the banisters, her dark eyes snapping with vivacity. "Hey, pop, don't forget we're going to the zoo tomorrow."

"Don't address your father as 'hey,' " said Doris, "and it depends on how you behave tonight. You make any trouble, young lady, and you'll go nowhere tomorrow."

"Well, gee whillikers, I won't make any trouble. We're going, aren't we, Daddy?"

And Brade found himself with no alternative but to say yes. "If it doesn't rain," he added.

"Actually," said Brade, afterward, "I'm not so sure that I can, Doris."

"What?" called Doris from the kitchen as the dishwasher let loose with a suctioning splash. She came into the living room. "What did you say?"

"I said I don't know that I can go to the zoo tomorrow."

"Why not?"

"Cap Anson will be coming over."

Doris frowned and took off her apron. "How was that arranged?"

"Simply enough. He said he would come and I couldn't say no."

"Why not? It's easy enough to pronounce."

"I couldn't. Not to Cap Anson. You know how he is."

"I know. But knowing isn't necessarily liking. It's his book, not yours. Why should you sweat over it so?"

"Because it's going to be a good book once it's done; an important book. Actually, I'm rather proud of being able to help out."

"Well, he'll have to come some other time."

"I've disappointed him twice already, Doris."

"Twice?"

"Last night was once. I had a definite appointment to meet him at five, and you know the way he insists on appointments being kept to the minutes. And I wasn't there."

Doris shrugged and began glancing through the copy of *TV Guide*. "That was scarcely a tragedy for him. He delivered his material to Virginia."

"I know. But he was dreadfully disappointed, for sure, and shocked. He considers impunctuality a personal affront."

"He seemed perfectly normal," said Doris, unimpressed. "I saw him through the screen door, giving

Ginny the envelope, and he didn't look the least shocked."

"Well, he was disappointed, whether he showed it or not. Then this morning he was in my office at ten, right after lecture, and I hadn't read the material, and he *was* disappointed that time."

"Don't you think it was a little unreasonable of him to expect life to continue undisturbed after one of your students has died in an accident?" She stressed the final phrase ever so faintly.

"Of course it was unreasonable, but he's an old man and chemistry is his life. What happened to Ralph meant nothing to him, so when Cap calmly said he would be here at the house tomorrow morning, I couldn't say no."

"Just the same, you'll have to take Virginia. She's been looking forward to it all week. And don't you say that I can take her. I've a mountain of wash that I've put off exactly long enough."

"Look," said Brade, "I'll call Cap tonight and suggest he come at nine. There's no point in taking Ginny earlier than eleven. It will be too cold, most likely, earlier than that, and that would give me two hours with him."

Doris made no direct answer to that. She turned on television and said, wearily, "It's a tired variety show and I'm not in the mood to watch it and I *am* in the mood to watch something."

"What's on the other channels?"

"Oh, Lord, a basketball game and a revivalist and an old picture I've seen before."

She sat down with a bag of knitting and focussed unhappily on the television screen. She did not knit. Brade was certain she wasn't watching, either.

She spoke finally, obviously annoyed with herself at no longer being able to ignore the subject, "Is there anything new about Ralph?"

Brade looked up from Cap Anson's manuscript. (He would have gone downstairs to his basement workroom if he had not, to put it baldly, needed company, even that of an unhappy Doris.)

He said, "The policeman was at my office today."

She looked up at once, beautiful eyes wide. "What!"

"Just to return the key to the lab; the one Ralph had had; but it made me nervous the way he looked about."

"Did he *say* anything?"

"If you mean did he say anything about murder, no."

"Well, then, aren't you going to forget about it, too? Can't you leave it alone."

"Even if it *was* murder?"

"It's done. One rather unpleasant boy is dead. You won't bring him back to life."

"It's not all over and done with. There is a girl who apparently loved him and was going to marry him. There's a mother who, I understand, had a great deal of tragedy in her life and who went through much to educate him. It's not all over. It's not done with."

"It won't do them any good for you to get into trouble."

"I *am* in trouble. I've been thinking all day how to get *out* of trouble."

"No one suspects murder except you."

"And how long will it stay that way? One person today wondered how Ralph could possibly have mistaken sodium cyanide for sodium acetate. She was pretty much in a state of shock, but she'll calm down eventually and start wondering about it seriously. Other chemists about the place might begin wondering. Someone will eventually go to the police. Do you want that particular sword of Damocles over our heads?"

"Who's this 'she' you're talking about?"

"Roberta Goodhue. She's the girl who was going to marry Ralph."

Doris said at once, desperately, intuitively, "Maybe *she* did it. Maybe he was throwing her over."

Brade said, "I've thought of exactly that. I've thought of a number of things." He put down the sheet of manuscript he had been holding in his hand. "Doris. Listen."

She said, "What?"

"Let me go over this with you. Must I carry it alone? Maybe you'll see something I don't see. For God's sake, maybe you'll see a way out."

Doris bent her head over her unknitted knitting. "All right. If you must talk about it, talk about it."

He said, "I thought I'd get things organized on paper. That was my first impulse, you know. Make up lists. Be orderly. But I thought: what if someone finds the scrap, finds the pieces in the wastebasket, or finds ashes and wonders what I've been burning. I mean, it's that kind of uncertainty I'm living with now. It's—it's unbearable."

He went on, "In the first place, if we grant it's murder, we've got to decide who it can be. I told you last night it would have to be someone who knew chemistry and knew Ralph's research methods. That makes me the obvious suspect, but if you leave me out of account, who else can it be? There *is* one other person with access to Ralph's laboratory and the opportunity to watch his work in detail."

"Who?"

"Gregory Simpson, Ralph's lab partner. He says Ralph never said a word to him and maybe that's true, but Simpson could still watch Ralph working. He could see Ralph prepare flasks of acetate and put them away in his desk.

"No one else had quite that chance, but others, Charlie Emmett, or any of the students, or Cap Anson, for that matter, who are around that part of the floor might have observed the same thing. Or it's theoretically possible that someone could have gotten into Ralph's laboratory when he was out and gone through his notebooks and learned enough to figure out the plan of attack. But none of that is very likely, you see.

"As far as the murder method is concerned, it implicates me far and away the best. Simpson is a not-too-close second. Other people on the floor are outside possibilities. Anyone else is infinitesimal."

Doris said, "Why do you say that Simpson is a not-too-close second. It seems to me that he has every bit the opportunity you had."

"He's only twenty-two and there's no motive."

"No motive *you* know of, but you're not God. For that matter, you don't have a motive."

"Now in that connection there's something that bothers me. Now that he's dead and I've been asking questions—"

Doris frowned at once. "Why have you been asking questions, Lou? That's the worst thing you could do."

"I've been very discreet. And people have been telling me things without my asking questions, too. In any case, it seems he disliked me or feared me or both. I'm not quite certain."

"Why should he have disliked you?"

"Apparently, he dislikes people easily. I don't know

why me, particularly; or why he should be afraid of me. It doesn't matter. Whatever his reasons, it may be something that the police could work up into a motive. They might say that I'd done a lot for the boy, or felt that I had and here he showed ingratitude, running me down to others. So in a fit of anger I do him in."

"That's mad."

"The police might think I'm mad. I've lost my temper at times. I've been known to yell at my students when they do something particularly silly-ass. I would have half-killed Ralph if the cyanide business had really been an accident, and he had managed to survive. Everyone knows that I can show temper."

"So can anyone," said Doris. "Surely there must be someone with a better motive than the ability to lose one's temper at times."

"There is one, at that. Jean Makris."

"Oh? What's her motive?"

Brade told her.

Doris said, "You have a sexy little hell-hole at the university, it seems."

Brade shrugged. "It does seem so, doesn't it? Anyway, Jean Makris has the motive, but she doesn't have the knowledge."

"How much knowledge does it take to switch powders?"

"It's not just knowledge. It's confidence, too. I imagine a non-chemist would even be afraid to handle cyanide; afraid the poison would get in through the fingertips. Roberta, on the other hand, would have both motive and the necessary knowledge if she were being thrown over, as you say. However, we have no reason to think that she was being thrown over.

"Of course," Brade went on, wearily, "there are motives we don't know about, again as you say. Ranke certainly disliked the boy intensely. The question is, how intensely? Is there something about their to-do we don't know? Foster nearly flunked him. Was there anything there we know nothing about?"

Doris said (she was beginning to knit), "I wouldn't worry about motive, if I were you. No one liked him. You'll find motive enough anywhere you look."

"Motive, yes, but motive *enough?* Good God, if we killed people we just didn't like or even just couldn't stand, we'd depopulate Earth among the lot of us. No, there's no use considering petty motives."

"Nonsense," said Doris. "Don't start eliminating people too easily and finding yourself left with only yourself as suspect. Petty motives probably cause most of the murders in the world. I'm sure of it."

"Well."

"Don't brush me off that way, Lou. I know what I'm saying." She pulled at the yarn, and was knitting at racing speed now. "You might have included one person in your list of those who disliked Ralph Neufeld; someone with a petty dislike over a petty incident, yet someone who could have murdered him cheerfully as a result of it."

Brade was startled. "Who?"

Doris yanked savagely at the yarn, which had caught in a tangle. "Me."

10

NATURALLY, Brade's first impulse was to laugh, but though he did not and confined himself merely to an incredulous and explosive, "You," Doris said at once, "Don't laugh. I mean it."

"I'm not laughing and you can't mean it."

"Surely you remember Ralph was here at the house last Christmas. Remember?"

"With the other students, yes. We invited them all," he said, remembering. "The time your vase was broken."

"You remember that, too? Well, then, do you remember exactly how it was broken?"

Brade shrugged. "Ralph broke it." It was half a guess. It was the answer that fit the context of the conversation.

Doris looked at him balefully, as though transferring to his person the memory of that dire event. "It's the way he broke it. It was my own vase, Lou. I made it at the pottery class."

"I *know*, Doris."

But it was a grievance that would not be shunted aside. "It was the only nice thing I managed to get out of it. The shape was just right and the colors were glazed just right and it was my own. I didn't buy it, I made it." She had put her knitting down in her lap again. "And I told them about it and showed it to them. I showed them my initials on the bottom."

"I remember that," said Brade, not quite daring to show his impatience. That vase had remained in the house for the better part of a year and during that time it had been the conversation piece of every gathering. Doris had always been pseudo-bashful about it and had made jokes over its slight asymmetry, but she had the fierce pride in it that essentially non-creative persons always seem to work up over a more or less fortuitous piece of creation.

Doris said, "Ralph Neufeld stood near that end table." She pointed to the end table near the large armchair. There was nothing on it now, had been nothing since the time of the vase, and Brade was suddenly aware of that as a gesture of mourning.

"He stood there and his elbow moved just a bit and down it went in a million pieces." She was staring at the empty place on the floor, seeing it again, no doubt, in all its brokenness. "I tried for days to put it together again, glue it. I couldn't. There were too many pieces."

Brade said, uneasily, "Accidents will happen."

"It was no accident, and it's time you knew that. I haven't said anything because I didn't want to embarrass your relations with him at school. But he's dead now and I can say it. It was no accident. I happened to be looking at him at the time. I saw his elbow move. There was no reason for it to move. He wasn't reaching for anything. He hadn't been startled. His elbow just moved quietly backward just far enough.

"And he didn't jump. Everyone else jumped or cried out at the crash, but not he. He knew it was coming, you see. He just calmly looked behind him and down at the vase and stepped away. He didn't say he was sorry; then or ever. He just smiled a bit. He actually smiled. It had made him happy to make me miserable."

Brade shook his head. "You're making more of it—"

"I'm telling you exactly what happened." Her eyes were hot, but dry. "And I tell you this, Lou; to some people it might have been nothing, just a broken vase. But for me it was motive for murder. If I had had a knife in my hand at that moment, Lou, I would have stabbed him to the heart and been glad. I would have killed him."

Brade tried to keep all emotion out of his voice. "You think you would, perhaps. But if the knife had been in your hands, you wouldn't have."

"Oh, no. Don't fool yourself, Lou. I would have."

"There were other things you might have done, Doris. You might have gone into hysterics, screamed at him, beaten him. You did none of that. As I remember, you remained in complete control and were the perfect hostess. You said your goodbyes nicely when the time came and it was only afterward—"

"I said no good-bye to him."

"Nevertheless you retained control. And if you could keep from screaming, you could keep from killing."

"No. Screaming would have done no good. It was not what I wanted. I'll tell you how I feel about him. When I heard he was dead, I was glad. I was sorry and worried because it meant we were involved, but that's all. It's almost a year later, and I haven't forgiven him, and I still think he deserves being dead. Any person who would do what he did that night has filled many lives with his malice probably."

"All right, Doris," said Brade, trying to break it off. "You're not proving anything."

"I'm not? I'm trying to show you, Lou, that you don't know anything about motives. You don't know what can make one person kill and not another. Why should you? It's not your field. You would laugh yourself sick if a detective, even a very clever one, walked into your laboratory and tried to tell you how to run your research. Then why should you think you can be a detective just because you're a chemist? You don't have the experience or the know-how and you're only making trouble for yourself. So stop it. *Stop* it."

Brade was silent.

Doris said, "Let it be an accident, Lou, and if someone killed him, that's all right, too. You're not God. It's not up to you to punish."

Brade turned away. He mumbled, "I have to call Cap."

Brade spent two poor and rather miserable hours with Anson's manuscript. This portion dealt with the early years of the career of J. J. Berzelius, the Swedish chemist who, in his day, was absolute tyrant of chemistry. He made basic contributions to half a dozen branches of the science, discovered several elements, invented the term "catalysis," worked out the chemical symbols still used to this day and so on.

Above all other chemists, he was Anson's hero, and Brade wondered, as he read, how much unconscious identification there was between Anson and Berzelius on the part of the former. Of course no man could, in the first half of the twentieth century, wield the power that Berzelius had in the nineteenth. The science had grown too big.

And yet—Berzelius had also watched his day dying before his own death. He had invented the radical theory of organic chemistry and had stuck to it with fervor and faith until it persisted in the face of accumulating contradictory data only by virtue of his own support. The more correct structural notions of organic chemistry nevertheless gained steadily during Berzelius' old age and took over, undisputed, with his death.

Did Anson see himself in that, too? Did he see himself as the last great proponent of "ball-and-peg" chemistry before the quantum mechanics boys took over with their resonance and their *pi* electrons?

Brade put aside the manuscript at last, feeling depressed and worn out. Doris came through to make mention of a few neutral subjects, such as that of making certain an extra bottle of milk was left in the box the next morning. Thereafter, Brade made sure the doors were locked and the various kitchen appliances were turned off and went upstairs to bed.

He fell asleep without trouble, but it was a restless sleep and filled with confused dreams.

Then he found himself staring into his pillow and knew from the stillness and darkness that it was as yet nowhere near dawn. He lifted his head just enough to catch sight of the illuminated dial of the small alarm clock on the night table. It was ten after three.

He turned his pillow over and put his head carefully down on the cool side. Then he carefully arranged his arms and legs in what seemed a relaxed position. Slowly, he closed his eyes—

It wouldn't help. He was awake.

He dreaded this. It happened when he was troubled, more so in recent years. Something, some trifling discomfort of his sleeping position, some petty noise from outside, might wake him some time between two and four.

And then he would lie awake, and his worries would grow and come to seem insurmountable.

He could fight it at times; he knew what a fraud and hoax it was. He knew that with morning and sunlight the most terrible night fears would shrink and shrivel. There were times when he could deliberately turn his mind to the design of an experiment or to the construction of a lecture. There were times when he could take a book to the bathroom and read his wakefulness away.

And there were times when he lacked the spirit for any defense at all and simply lay there, overwhelmed.

Doris was sleeping heavily. The street light made its way through the slats of the Venetian blinds and the curtains just enough to bring her face into something more than shadow and less than features.

She always slept on her side, he himself on his stomach, and Brade wondered why people assumed the sleeping positions they did; why one position was comfortable to one person and painful to another; whether it was mere custom begun in babyhood or whether there was a physical distinction in the distribution of blood vessels and nerve endings.

For a moment, he tried to hold on to that, to imagine experiments, to work out mock theories that would lull him to sleep—like another man counting sheep—but it all slipped away.

The thought occurred to him: I wonder if she's dreaming of her vase.

The vase and the elbow. Why should Ralph have done that? If he had deliberately and maliciously broken the vase, was it because he knew it meant much to Doris and was irreplaceable? Was it so that he could hurt her, and through her, Brade? Was it an expression of Ralph's hate for Brade?

How long had Ralph been a student of Brade's at that time? It was last Christmas and he had been working with Brade for perhaps half a year. He did not know Doris. He had never seen her before. It could not have been her he was trying to hurt.

Only Brade. It was Brade he had hated, and Jean Makris was right.

But then what was the motive of the hate?

People spoke so freely of motives, as though they were simply designed mathematical forces, pulling this way and that, in plain view, predictable, capable of analysis.

But they weren't. It was as Doris had said and tried to show. They were dark and hidden things; unrecognizable and complicated. What was motive to one was not motive to another just as a comfortable sleeping position to one was sheer pain to another.

How could he untangle such a snarl? He could not as much as recognize the motivations of the wife he saw every day. He recognized the craving for security and understood some of the things it made her do. But he had missed completely the connection between a broken vase and a nearly uncontrollable blood lust.

For that matter, what motivated Brade himself? What ran Brade and made him go? What if the police said: Brade, you are a murderer. You have a motive.

How could he defend himself against that? Did he know his own motives? What if they said that he did it because of Doris' vase? How could he say no? Doris said she would kill for it, and they would say that she had made him do the job for her and that for nearly a year— for nearly a year—for nearly a year (his thoughts were

becoming thick) for nearly a year they had plotted together to make him—Ralph—rebuild the vase or else—
they would choke—the poison—down the thro. . . .

He was awake again at seven before the alarm had a
chance to ring. He remembered waking during the night
but could not recall the nature of his thoughts.

Except that it was something about the broken vase.

He had dreamed about it, a dream broken just now at
the moment of waking. It had been standing on the end
table, as it had once, except that hair-line marks showed
all over it where the pieces joined and Doris yelled at him
not to touch it because the glue had not hardened yet. Except that the cement lines were red—like blood.

And he had awakened.

It wasn't until he was halfway through his quick morning shower that the vase finally left his mind.

Cap Anson, in accordance with Brade's phone call of
the evening before, arrived precisely at the stroke of nine,
and Brade, who had breakfasted and was himself ready
by then, let him in through the door that led directly into
his basement study.

Anson put his cane down and lowered himself into one
of the two chairs. He said, "How did you get along with
old Berzelius, Brade?"

Brade forced a smile. "Self-assured fellow."

"He had the right to be. He was made a baron, you
know."

"Oh, was he?"

"I discuss it in a later chapter. It was his wedding day.
He was married late in life to a girl thirty years younger
than himself, and the king of Sweden made him a baron
as a wedding present. I go into that in detail. I see no rea-

son why a history of organic chemistry should not also be a history of organic chemists."

Brade wasn't sure what was best to say. Anson had certainly separated chemistry from chemists in his own life. His own personal life had never been allowed to impinge upon his work.

It was known that there had been a Mrs. Anson once and that she was dead now and that Anson lived in lonely quarters with a housekeeper taking care of him. It was known that he had a married daughter living somewhere in the Midwest with children of her own.

He never spoke of any of them. There was no suggestion of estrangement. He just never talked of them because they had nothing to do with chemistry.

Brade said, "Where personal matters have an application to the course of organic chemistry, they should be discussed. For instance, being made a baron is a measure of the value put on Berzelius' career by the society of the time. Organic chemistry was becoming sufficiently important to everyday life to warrant the ennoblement of an organic chemist."

Anson nodded slowly. "A good point. Thank you. Now I have cut out some paragraphs on the discovery of selenium. That, and the whole business of blowpipe analysis is, of course, extremely interesting, but it isn't organic chemistry."

"I agree," said Brade. "The book will be quite long enough even so."

"Good. Now would you look at page 82. I haven't yet got to the radical theory but this seems the logical place—"

They went on in this manner, heads together, manuscript pages lifted and replaced, pushed away and pulled back, until Doris' voice called out, artificially soft in deference to Anson's presence. "Lou, I think Virginia is about ready for you."

Brade looked up. "All right, Doris. Well, Cap, I think we've done most of what we've set out to do. Shall we let it go now till next time?"

Anson said, "Are you going somewhere?"

"I'm taking Ginny to the zoo. She's going to have to write some sort of composition for her English class this next week, and this will give her subject matter and a good time, I hope, *and* a rest for her mother. Kill three birds with one stone." He smiled briefly and stood up, pushing the pages of the chapter together and putting the stapler on top of them as a paperweight.

Anson gathered up his own material. "Would you object to my coming with you? There is more to discuss."

"Well," Brade hesitated and did not know how to refuse the mild request. "It will be dull for you."

Anson smiled sadly. "Most things are dull at my age." He took his cane.

It was a mild, sunny day, unseasonably warm. With what seemed almost a summer sun, there was yet the lack of summer crowds and Brade thought with minimal satisfaction that at least so much had broken right. Ginny was inside the monkey house while Brade and Anson sat on a bench outside.

Brade stared absently at the cage set up on a tall stilt in the middle of a circular plot of grass, containing within it one old golden eagle that retained yet a sleepy fierceness in its small yellow eyes. He wondered how long the bird had been imprisoned and what it had done on some cosmic scale of crime and punishment that had warranted its imprisonment.

Anson had bought himself a bag of popcorn and, with his cane laid across his legs, was crunching the soft kernels with an obvious pleasure.

He said, "I talked with Littleby yesterday afternoon, Brade."

"Oh?"

"He was telling me about the safety lectures he had been planning. Of course, the old fraud has convinced himself by now that he really has been planning them all along."

"Yes, I know." Brade wasn't really interested.

"And then he asked about you."

Brade sat up, back suddenly stiff. "About *me?*"

"That's why I brought you out here. Away from Mrs. Brade, you know!"

"What did he say?"

"Nothing specific. Nothing right out. The idea I got, however, is that your appointment will be renewed for one final year the next time it comes up. You'll be put on a year's notice to find a new job."

11

THE temperature seemed to drop and the sun, shining directly down on Brade's shoulders, gave no warmth.

Cap Anson's voice was coming from far off and the homely sounds of people holidaying in the park dropped away into distance.

Brade's first concern was not with the breaking of the long rod of livelihood; not with the wrenching of an accustomed way of life out of socket. It was Doris.

She had predicted this. As long as he was without tenure, he had been at the mercy of Littleby, or of any new department head who might succeed him.

Brade had maintained stubbornly that it would not happen. His family position lay in its not happening.

How would he now face Doris?

It did not occur to him that Cap Anson might be wrong; that he might have misinterpreted Littleby. Anson's conclusion jibed too well with Brade's uneasy interpretation of Littleby's coldness of yesterday morning; which after all had been the morning of the afternoon on which Littleby had spoken to Anson.

Brade said, "Was this because of the m—" He stopped.

He had almost said "murder." He tried again. "Because what happened to Ralph Neufeld?"

Anson looked puzzled. "You mean Ralph's accident?"

"Yes."

"He said nothing about that. Why should there be a connection?"

Brade shrugged and looked away.

Anson said, "It's a matter of research results. You're not publishing enough."

"Publish or perish," said Brade, bitterly.

"Well, you know that, Brade. It's an old story. It's a man's reputation that holds his value to the university. A man's reputation is built up out of his contributions of scientific research. His contributions are measured by the number of publications he puts out."

Brade said, "Then if I were to take my findings, scrabble them together, and dole them out in skimpy paragraphs to this journal and that; if I were to make a dozen publications out of each piece of research; I would end up a great man, I suppose. It seems a man's reputation can be measured by the number of thin slivers into which he can divide his research."

"Brade, Brade." The old chemist listed a quieting hand, gnarled and veined, and patted Brade's knee. Don't make an issue of quality over quantity. The papers you have put out in the last ten years have been careful and worthwhile, but scarcely transcendent contributions." He almost chuckled in appreciation of the phrase and repeated, "Scarcely transcendent contributions."

"I've had scarcely transcendent students," said Brade, pettishly, and was ashamed almost at once. There was no point in shifting blame.

But Anson said, "True enough. Whose fault is that?"

"What do you want me to do? Scrabble for grants so that I can buy myself students? I'm not going to. I made up my mind long ago, Cap, that I wasn't going hat in hand to Washington with some project designed to extract government money. I'm not cutting my research into strange designs to suit what is currently fashionable. I am investigating what interests me and that's all. If that's worth a public contribution, I'll take it with no strings attached. If it isn't, that's all right, too." He put anger into it, justifying himself in his own mind, hearing once again the practical arguments that condemned him as a fool who equated poverty with virtue and thought prosperity sin.

Anson said. "Oh, come. You know what I think of this grant binge we're on. I'm not suggesting that. But why are you so upset? Can't you find another job?" He fixed Brade with a sharp, unwavering stare.

Brade had trouble meeting it. What could he say? Could he say there was a negative feedback involved; that the absence of promotion made promotion necessarily absent; that after so many years as assistant professor, questions naturally arose in connection with any proposal for promotion?

Why has he been an assistant professor so long? What is wrong with the man that he hasn't been promoted before this?

And the promotion then waits on the answer to the questions.

And after each year of non-promotion the questions are louder and more insistent and harder to answer. After a while, there just is no answer.

Then, in finding a new job, the same questions would arise. It wasn't that he was too old to find a new job, or too poor a chemist; he had just been frozen too long in his status.

Brade had a quick vision of the polite interviews, of the polite tours of chemistry departments, of the polite handshakes of department members, of the polite discussion of my research, your research, of the polite exchanges of reprints, of more politeness than could be stomached.

And all the politeness would amount to the fact that no one would be so impolite as to ask the one question that counted: Why have you been an assistant professor so long, Professor Brade? Why is your school letting you go rather than promote you?

Can you answer: They won't promote me because they haven't promoted me. They are letting me go because they are tired and embarrassed at not promoting me.

He was still trying to meet Anson's gaze.

Anson said, "I can use my influence, you know, to help."

What influence, thought Brade with helpless bitterness. Oh, Cap, Cap, what influence? You have influence here at school because you're a living ghost no one likes to offend? But where else? They worship only the real Anson elsewhere; the real Anson, now dead, who once made mighty contributions to organic chemistry. The old man who calls himself Anson is an imposter with only a physical connection through time to the real Anson; the soul, the influence, is gone.

Anson said, "Or if you'd rather stay at the university, then *make* them keep you, by God. You have till June before they commit themselves to giving you notice. Do something by then."

"Do something," repeated Brade. "Do what?"

And Anson pounded his cane on the gravel walk so

that it crunched and threw up a small spray of small stones. "Are you giving up? Fight, man. You're not in the university to vegetate. Science is a fight." He clenched his old fist.

But I *am* in a university to vegetate, old man. There are fights enough in the world where you can be well paid for fighting. I am not here to fight.

Ginny came dashing out of the monkey house. Her straight, dark hair was in two tight pigtails that went flying backward out of contact with her brown sweater, and her low-heeled shoes kicked up gravel at each step.

"Daddy, is it all right if I go to the reptile house?"

Brade looked up with a flashing moment of non-recognition of his daughter. He said, "Yes, of course. Where is it?"

"Right over there. See the sign."

"Do you want us to come with you, Ginny?" He reached out for her, wanting suddenly, very hard, to take her in his arms and hug her and comfort her so that the feel of a small creature accepting comfort from him might, in turn, comfort him.

But unaware, and looking only at the entrance to the reptile house, she stepped out of reach, and said, "I can go myself. I'll come back after a while."

And she skipped away, eleven years old and perfectly self-sufficient.

Brade said, "What about the work Ralph was doing?"

"The kinetic studies?" Anson made a displeased face and shook his head violently. "Forget that."

"*Forget it?* Why, it opens up a whole new field of possibilities in organic reactions. If I could put the finishing touches on it, the final confirmations," (suddenly, he was talking himself into renewed hope), "I could put out a paper that would make an astonishing splash."

But no answering spark seemed to be struck in Anson. He said, "How do you intend to finish up this uncompleted work? A new student couldn't get a Ph.D. out of a finishing touch."

"Well, no."

"Do you intend to do the work yourself, Brade?"

Brade didn't answer. He scuffed gravel away with his shoe, leaving a patch of packed dirt.

Anson said, "You don't have the background for that sort of work. I know." He shook his head. "If you had come to me before starting this type of thing, I would have warned you off. No professor should start his students on research work that is over his own head. I always made it a practice to know and understand exactly what my students were doing. If one of them had suddenly vanished, I could always have carried on his experiments myself. Now you're not in that position, are you?"

Brade flushed. He had dutifully looked at the duplicate sheets given him by Ralph, but its integrations and its calculations of configurational entropy had been well beyond his own understanding.

Brade said, "I suppose I could learn. I'm not too proud to learn."

"It's not pride. You don't have time. Let me tell you what to do." Anson put his hand softly on Brade's shoulder so that for a moment Brade was keenly aware that his relations to this old man were those of his own students to himself. "If I were you, I would break new ground. I would find a field that was so new, so thinly occupied, that I could not help but make startling discoveries; one that the boys on grants had not yet invaded. Look at that eagle!"

Brade looked up, startled. The bird's eyes were closed, its wings folded. Slowly, its beak opened and closed, as though it were an old man, mumbling in his sleep.

Brade said, "What about it?"

"Well, it's carnivorous, for one thing. It eats meat. The monkey inside that house may eat insects but mostly they eat fruit and other vegetable food. Yet the vegetarian monkeys are closely related to carnivorous man, while the carnivorous eagle is not. How does this reflect in the chemistry of the three creatures?"

Brade said, "What's all this about?"

"I'm talking about comparative biochemistry. The chemical differences among species of organisms. The few people in it know very little of organic chemistry. You would have a special knowledge that would enable you to go far, eh? And it should be fascinating." He pointed to the reptile house. "What are the digestive adaptations, chemically speaking, of the python who eats an entire animal without chewing it, then spends days digesting it and perhaps months before eating again?"

"Good Lord, Cap," said Brade, smiling despite himself. "I wouldn't know where to begin."

"That's exactly it. Make your own trail."

"No, Cap. No. It doesn't strike a chord. I'm just not attracted to animal work."

Anson frowned. "If you did this, Brade, I'm sure I could talk Littleby into forgetting any notions he might have about terminating your appointment; at least to give you a decent chance on a new project. He might even promote you on the strength of it. It's not impossible."

"Thanks, Cap, but even so—"

"Are you afraid of something just because it's new?"

"No, but I've got to be interested, and I think it's kinetics I'm interested in now. I'll try to follow up Ralph's work myself. I'll try."

Anson rose. "I'll go now, Brade. You're making a mistake."

Brade looked after the departing figure with emotions so mixed he could scarcely separate the strands of feeling that made up the whole.

Poor fellow. He was obviously furious. He was still dispensing problems, still dictating areas of research. Of course, he hated kinetics and reaction mechanisms. It was the very thing that had outdated him.

Comparative biochemistry?

Brade looked up at the eagle and thought: What about it?

He felt a small pull, but it was only the pull of Cap Anson's promise to speak up for him. And that was a fallacious pull because Anson could not really sway Littleby. Brade was sure of that. Only Anson himself really believed in his own powers any longer.

Now Ralph's problem—

Brade tried to recapture that small bud of hope he had experienced moments before but it was elusive. Surely, if he read Ranke's book on kinetics—

But he had seen the book often enough to know it would mean hard work; perhaps harder work than he could manage.

He sat on the bench, waiting for Ginny, and feeling very alone.

They returned home, Brade and Ginny, at close to four and already there was an atmosphere of get-ready about Doris and the house. Doris had used the relative freedom involved in the absence of husband and daughter in vacuuming and arranging, so that the house had a faintly unreal look.

She herself was in the phase of gathering disarray that would continue to gather until just before the conclusion of matters when it would somehow all get itself tied into a neat and tidy bundle and she would be ready to leave.

Doris cast them a busy look and said to Ginny, "Good time, Virginia?"

"Fine," said Ginny, condensing an elaborate six hours into a monosyllable.

"What did you eat for lunch?"

Ginny ticked them off on her fingers. "Umm, I had two hot dogs, and some ice cream and a box of crackerjacks and a bottle of soda and a bag of peanuts and—and— that's all."

"That's *all*." Doris was horrified. "How do you feel?"

Ginny blinked. "I'm not hungry," she confessed.

Doris said to her husband, "Did *you* eat anything?"

"Oh, don't worry about me."

"Why not? You look awful. What happened? Or did *you* eat two hot dogs and some ice cream and a dozen varieties of garbage along with Virginia? Why didn't you buy her a regular lunch? All she'll be able to eat for supper will be a laxative."

"She'll be all right," said Brade. "Children are like ostriches. Besides they have a right to a stomach ache or two."

"Oh, my philosopher friend," said Doris, dryly, "except that you're not the one who has to sit up with her at night. Now you've got to shave and see that your brown shoes with the plastic soles are polished. I've laid out your suit and your shirt and at 5:30 you go and get Nadine to sit with Virginia. Are you *sure* you've eaten? You look pasty to me. What happened?"

Brade said, "I'm afraid I offended Cap."

"That's a terrible thing," said Doris, sniffing. "That's worth ruining at least a whole day over. What have you done now?"

"He was advising me as to the future course of my research," said Brade cautiously, "and I didn't quite go along with him."

"Well, you're not his student anymore. It's time he realized that."

"Yes, I suppose so."

Doris sat down. She was in her slip and her hair was in curlers. She paused to light a cigarette, then said, "Is that all?"

"Is that all what?"

"Is that all that happened?"

Brade hesitated fractionally and then said, firmly, "Nothing else happened and don't start a regular cross-examination."

"You don't seem particulary keen on tonight's affair."

"I never have been, Doris. When have I ever pretended otherwise? It's a boring necessity and you know it."

"Why don't you make a virtue of necessity, then, and talk to Littleby today?"

"About what?"

"About what do you suppose? About being promoted."

Brade passed his tongue over his lips. "Doris, it can't be done. For one thing, you can't discuss administrative business at this sort of get-together. Secondly, it's not the sort of thing you can discuss, anyway."

"Not the sort of thing *you* can discuss."

"Besides," finished Brade, lamely, "this is not a good time. With Ralph's poisoning—"

Doris said, "Is there anything about that you haven't told me? Anything new?"

Brade was startled. "No. Nothing."

"Are you sure?"

"Yes."

And in apparent *non sequitur,* Doris said, "Foster called."

"Foster? *Our* Foster?"

"Professor Merrill Foster, who teaches the graduate course you should be teaching. Is that sufficient identification?"

"All right, Doris, please. I'm not in the mood to play at sarcasm with you. Foster called. Leave it at that. What did he want?"

"He wanted to speak to you."

"About what, for heaven's sake."

"He wouldn't say. He seemed quite annoyed that I had answered and very anxious to be certain that you would be at Littleby's place tonight. I said you would be."

"Hmm. What do you suppose he wants?"

"I don't know exactly, but I can tell you this. He sounded awfully chipper about it. He had that little undercurrent of excitement, you know. So, knowing Foster, I should judge that what he has for you, Lou, is bad news."

12

BAD news? What other kind was turned out these days? Was it the same bad news that Cap Anson had already brought him, corroborated now, polished to a luster, neatly packaged for delivery?

But Brade maintained his poise somehow. He said, "Don't get ravenish, Doris. If it's Foster, it can be anything, a new dirty story he's heard, probably. And now I have half an hour for a nap, so let it go."

He took off his shirt, pants and shoes and lay down, but did not nap. Instead, he smoldered into slow anger. He could understand Littleby discussing the matter with Cap Anson. Anson was the elder statesman of the department, the distinguished figurehead, and the original sponsor of Brade, besides. But to discuss it with Foster—

"Handies" Foster, Brade thought with sudden viciousness.

He stared at the ceiling as though it were a white screen taking the film of his memories as it unreeled. He remembered the first day he had ever seen Foster. Foster was just a kid then, a youngster in his late twenties, fresh out of one of the midwestern schools.

He had been led through the laboratories and was introduced to the faculty members and from the beginning he gave the effect of being big without being big physically. He exuded a kind of jovial self-confidence and knew everyone's field of research and discussed them all familiarly with, somehow, no sign of having boned up for the occasion though that was exactly what he must have done.

Brade had disliked him for his manner of seeming to own whatever patch of ground he rested his foot on. but had tried unceasingly to fight it even after Foster's relatively rapid advance in the department to a position equal to that of Brade.

Doris had disliked him intensely from the first. She said, "He's crude and I don't think he's funny."

He was crude, surely. His pet delight lay in his numerous off-color stories which, to give him his due he told with excellent techniques. He maintained an air of mock flirtatiousness which was constant and undiscriminating. He rolled his eyes ferociously at secretaries, technicians, and graduate students (female) alike. He had a way of placing his arm casually about the shoulders or waist of women he might be standing next.

There seemed to be no offense in it. At least no woman in Brade's experience had screamed or slapped him or complained to Littleby. And there were times when Brade wondered why this was so. Did Foster possess an animal magnetism visible (and pleasing) to females only?

It was with a certain delight then, that he had heard, quite by accident, that Merrill Foster had another first name by which he was known to every girl across the length and breadth of the chemistry building—"Handies" Foster.

Brade mouthed the name now soundlessly, "Handies" Foster. It seemed to degrade the man, put him in proper prospective.

Why did Littleby have to discuss the matter with him? If Brade were to be turned out, care might at least be taken of his dignity. He deserved that much at least.

He closed his eyes. If it came to that, then, if he were to be tumbled out of his place in such a way that all might jeer, he would find his own way to retaliate. In that moment, it seemed an easy and inevitable thing to learn what he needed to know in order to complete Ralph's work, to find another job, and to publish (by God) and revolutionize the science from the new institution. Let them share his glory—

He was drifting into the equivocal borderline between sleep and wakefulness, and plans for revenge distorted subtly and became fantastic, when Doris's voice cut across it all matter-of-factly, "I think it's time to dress."

Littleby lived in one of the older suburbs, one that kept its estates intact and guarded vigilantly against the invasion of the lower-middle-class housing projects, thus maintaining its social makeup and its low real estate tax.

Littleby had bought into the social structure some ten years back, and he owned now a house that retained the flavor of an antiquity that was quaint and not uncomfortable. Paneling and woodwork, stairways that were wide and rooms that were tall, yielded memories of a day when labor was cheap and unnecessary pains were the true sign of wealth.

Where the flavor of an older day might take on an unpleasant sharpness, the resources of modern science were called upon, so that the kitchen and bathrooms had been completely modernized in stainless steel and colored tile, and the spacious cellars bore the intrusion of washers, driers and other paraphernalia of contemporary cleanliness.

Mrs. Littleby met them just inside the door (in an older day, before the extinction of the race of personal servants, a butler would undoubtedly have done so). She was a short woman with none of the accepted stigmata of aristocracy. Her mousy-brown hair, which seemed to lack even the strength of will to turn gray, had been carefully arranged, but did not look it. Her eyes seemed made for glasses though she wore none and she wore a dress so formidably tasteless as almost to lend her an air of distinction.

She was always very kind and thoughtful of her guests, never forgot names or ranks or any recent mark of distinction. One could not help liking her for that reason alone.

She said, with a warm smile, "Professor Brade, how nice you could come. And Mrs. Brade, what a charming dress. If you would put hats and coats in the cloak room—And Professor Brade, I was most distressed to hear of the unfortunate accident to your student. As I said to the professor" (*the* Professor was, of course, her husband) "the young man, poor soul, was out of his misery, but what a trial it must be to those who were close to him and survived him, and a sponsoring professor is, in a way, like a member of the family, I always think. Why, I almost felt somehow that our little get-together ought to have been postponed but I know so many were counting on it—"

Brade mumbled polite agreements, smiling and nodding and sidling out of reach. Mrs. Littleby exchanged a few more words with Doris and then her attention was caught by new arrivals.

Brade heard Foster's voice immediately upon emerging from the cloak room. That was the way of Foster's voice. Without any advantage in decibels it managed to make itself heard over all competitors. There was a quality in his voice, something about its pitch or timbre, that yielded a special piercingness.

Foster stood near the hors d'oeuvres table and would, between sentences, idly and with half an eye, appraise the small bits of nourishment. Then he would choose a succulent one with the ease of long experience and lift it to his mouth. He had the knack of popping it in, chewing and swallowing it without seeming to miss a word.

Yardley and Gennaro, the two instructors, were his immediate audience, and this undoubtedly suited Foster. It was easier to dominate younger men, easier to direct the tone of a conversation and rule it.

Foster was saying, "The only other case I knew involved Wakefield of Southern Nebraska and he actually married his graduate student, his own Ph.D. candidate. He had five or six, but just this one girl and a pretty good-looker, not big enough upstairs for my taste, exactly, but all right. I was taking a summer course there so that's how I know about it.

"Wakefield was a bachelor, maybe forty then, not bad-looking, but a real bachelor, the kind you'd think would never get married. I mean, you were sure he never happened to come across a paper in any research journal describing the care and uses of girls, so he always just thought girls were boys who wore funny clothes."

He paused with the practiced air of one who knows

when to expect a laugh, and he wasn't disappointed. Maintaining an air of gravity himself, but obviously enjoying the appreciation, he picked up a cocktail glass and sipped at the contents.

"But, apparently," he went on, "he read some journals, not the chemical kind, I suppose, that did tell about girls. Or else, maybe a pal took him behind the barn and drew some pictures because all of a sudden, he invites the faculty over to his place for a cocktail party and announces an engagement and there's his student, blushing and smiling. And then they got married. I was at the wedding."

Gennaro said, "When was this, Merrill?"

Foster helped himself to a shrimp paste and pursed his plump lips thoughtfully. "Ten years ago. They're still married, last I heard. Now," he drew in a breath, as thought taking second wind, "what gets me is this: You have a girl student you think is a nice piece and you decide to play it legal and get married. O.K. But how do you get to that point? Someplace before you reach the preacher frame of mind you're wondering, maybe. Maybe this is good. Maybe this is the thing. How do you find out?"

"It seems to me," said Yardley, thoughtfully (he was a very earnest young man and a hesitant speaker who might, for that very reason, never make much of a lecturer), "there are many opportunities. They might attend seminars together and it could be natural that they have dinner together to discuss the status of her research."

"Oh, hell," said Foster, contemptuously, "you miss the point. I don't mean being together and talking. I mean, when does he give her that first squeeze? When does he kiss her and get hold of something? Listen, if she screams and starts yelling for the gendarmes, he's done for. Moral turpitude. Even tenure won't stand up against that. And then there's another risk. Suppose he tries messing about a little and doesn't like it. Well, there she is—still his student. How does he get rid of her? How does he—"

He interrupted himself at the approach of a thin dark girl, looking quite young, quite shy. Her voice was a murmur and Foster's own voice took on a sudden softness as though another man had entered his skin and spoken. He said, "Yes, dear," nodded, and the girl moved away.

Brade knew her, of course. Joan Foster, Merrill's wife, was as cool and gently refined as Foster himself was coarse and loud, and yet she never seemed annoyed by his behavior, and he never tempered his actions to her presence except in dealing with her directly.

Damnation, thought Brade with sudden revulsion, what devil drove the man to cultivate a lack of cultivation, to speak in an uneducated argot, to play the fool—when to everyone's sure knowledge he was highly educated, intensely cultured and a very bright chemist. With a wife like that, whom the very girls he manhandled knew he adored, why did he manhandle?

Womanhandle, thought Brade, and smiled despite himself. He could be as corny as Foster at times. Perhaps anyone could. Foster did it out loud. That was the difference.

Foster was saying, taking up where he left off, "Now the whole thing involves expert wolfing. What does a professorial babe in the woods know about wolfing? Or is it a case of fools rushing—" He happened to turn his head at an angle which caused his eyes to stumble over Brade. He cheered up instantly. "Hey, Lou, you been listening?"

"I heard you," said Brade, carefully.

"All right, then I leave it up to you. You're the expert. You're the ladies' man." He winked at the young instructors, who, in a battle of professors, forbore to take part by smiling. "Describe the moves in that particular chess game that would insure mate."

"If the problem," said Brade, "involves the interplay between a female student and a male professor and you don't know the techniques involved by experience, then no one on earth dares presume to know."

There was mild laughter, but Foster went into paroxysms. He slapped his thighs and shook his head. He reacted much more enthusiastically than necessary, of course, but that, Brade realized suddenly, was one of his secrets. He always laughed heartily at jokes at his own expense. That established the point that he could "take it," and gave him license to "dish it out."

The laughter, with long practice, might even be real laughter.

Foster recovered and began in a sudden confidential whisper, "By the way, Lou, got a minute?"

But Brade waved synthetically in courteous greeting to a blank space at the opposite end of the room and moved off with a mumbled, "Be seeing you, Merrill."

Foster was left with his whisper tumbling into a vacuum.

The room was filling up. After it had reached proper capacity, the double door leading to the main dining room would be opened, the two caterers currently engaged in setting up the comestibles would disappear and the guests would line up for their slices of ham and cheese, their meat balls and mounds of spaghetti, their baked beans and cole slaw. And later, their slivers of cake and cups of coffee.

Brade avoided Littleby as he walked the length of the room and the department head might have noticed him and might not. Brade thought the latter. Surely had Littleby seen him, the reflex action of a mechanical smile would have followed, whatever current circumstances.

Brade found himself near Otto Ranke and pretended to join the little group surrounding him. A quick glance backward showed that Foster wasn't following him.

Good! He simply was in no mood to be wept over and funeralized by the man who, after all, was going to profit by the whole deal. It was obvious there would be profit for this to Assistant Professor Merrill Foster. He was making a name for himself with speed. He was belligerent enough to push for associate much more crassly and baldly than Brade ever would. The only thing that could be balking Foster was the existence of the Brade block. Littleboy could be reluctant (or *say* he was reluctant) to push a junior man over Brade's head. With Brade out, Foster's promotion would be quickly forthcoming.

Brade shivered. The university was just a branch of the world after all. The ivy was no boundary where the jungle ceased. It was simply an imaginary line separating jungle from jungle with the worse jungle within, since the scholars in it had abandoned the world to avoid facing what they faced after all and were unequipped to deal with it.

Security? Brade noticed Doris speaking to Mrs. Gennaro, young and very polite, as suited the wife of an instructor. Probably not married long, perhaps not a college girl herself, in any case overwhelmed by the weight of dignity upon her. Did *she* find security in this?

He was growing aware of Ranke's sharply indignant voice. The physical chemist was addressing those about him with forceful heat. "What is cancer after all?" he was saying. "A disease. But what is a disease? There was a time when the learned scholars thought diseases due to an imbalance of humors within the body. When Pasteur said they were caused by micro-orgamisms parasitic on the human body, he was laughed at and scorned, but he was right, within his limits, after all. And mark this, he was not a physician, he was a chemist. The physicians laughed and had to be dragged into the pasture of truth by the unrelenting pull of circumstance.

"Now the physicians think of diseases as germs and viruses and it is time to put a finger through the rings in their noses and pull them by main force to a deeper truth. We already known that disease can be caused not only by the presence of a germ, but by the absence of a chemical. The absence of a food factor, like a vitamin, a particular amino acid or trace mineral; the congenital or acquired absence of a hormone or an enzyme, all lead to diseases of metabolism which are all the more important now that so many infectious diseases are under control.

"Good Lord, it is time for a new generalization. All diseases are due to the modification of the protein molecule. The modification may be due to faulty reproduction of a protein and then it is a mutation. It may be forced on the body by the absence of an essential building block. Another organism may invade the body and form modified proteins as viruses do, or produce toxins that modify proteins as bacteria do.

"What we must do is attack through the genetic code. All life is nucleoprotein and disease is inadequate nucleoprotein. To deal with the nucleoproteins" (his voice rose;

he was working himself into a rage), "we can't rely on biochemists. They don't know enough and certainly physicians are useless. The proteins must be studied by physical chemical techniques by men trained as the discipline of physical chemistry; and very advanced physical chemistry at that.

"Now I applied for a Public Health Service grant covering the detailed studies of proteins. I needed $200,000. That was high, yes, but I was proposing an important and extensive study. They're questioning it; they're trying to make do with $50,000. *Fifty thousand!* And why? Because the grant points out the usefulness of the studies in connection with the etiology of cancer. That automatically means it goes to the pathology boys for review. And what the hell do a bunch of pathologists know about cancer, will you tell me that? What the hell do—"

Brade turned away. The purpose might be different, but the attitude was not. It was that of an industrialist angling for government subsidy before expanding operations. It was no different—

He almost jumped at the sudden touch on his shoulder. He looked up. It was Foster, a look of gravity on his wide, florid face.

The younger man had a grip on Brade's sleeve. "Lou, listen. I've got to talk to you."

Brade forced a laugh. "You sound portentous. Bad news?"

"I don't know what to call it. I just thought you ought to know." He looked about uneasily, but no one was looking directly at them and his tentative pull at Brade's sleeve grew stronger. He lowered his voice. "It's about Ralph Neufeld."

"About Ralph?"

"Ssh. Listen, there's a detective or somebody going around asking questions? His name's Doheny. A little fat guy."

"What for? Why?"

"I don't know why. He hasn't talked to me. But he did talk to one of my boys and I got the word. The impression my boy got is that Doheny doesn't think Ralph's death was accidental."

13

BRADE stared at the younger man. He was caught completely off balance.

Foster mumbled uneasily, "Just thought you ought to know."

Brade shifted mental gears. He had spent hours associating Foster with additional news of dismissal, nothing more.

He tried to sound careless. He said, "How could Ralph's death be anything other than accidental?"

Foster said, "Well, you know, I think it's a little funny myself. It takes a novice to mistake cyanide and acetate. Your boy was no novice."

"Is that what the detective says?"

"Hell, Lou, I don't know what the detective says. But

he's been talking to my boy, as I told you, and asking if Ralph had been low in spirits, how his work was going, if he had said anything about troubles."

Mrs. Littleby interrupted with a tray of cocktails. Foster shook his head with a tight little smile, but Brade seized one with a quick wrist movement. He drank some of it, his eyes never leaving Foster's.

He said, "What are you trying to say, Merrill?"

Foster said, "I think the police suspect suicide."

Brade had expected the word, but it was shocking to hear it nevertheless. (Still suicide was better than murder, wasn't it? It was a way out, wasn't it?) He said, "Why suicide?"

"Why not?"

"His work was going well."

"So what? What do you know about his private life?"

"Do *you* know anything that would make suicide a tenable thought?"

Brade did not mean to sound belligerent about it but the strain of events was telling badly and his control was slipping.

Foster reacted at once. He hunched his eyebrows into hostility. "Look, don't jump on me. I'm just trying to do you a favor and warn you about this. If you want to kick about it, pardon *me* and make out like I said nothing."

"Why do you act as though it has something to do with me one way or the other," said Brade, with sharp and desperate indignation. "Even if it were suicide—"

And Ranke was suddenly between them, his eyes intent. "What's this about suicide?"

Brade looked at him sharply, speechlessly. Foster shrugged slightly as though to say, well, he had done his part and if Brade were going to shout about it he would have to take the consequences. Foster said, "We were just talking about Ralph Neufeld."

"Suicide?" Ranke's lips spread in a harpy-smile and his pointing finger ended an inch from the second button on Brade's shirt. "You know, I believe that. That boy was mad. Literally mad. We're lucky he didn't decide to take the chemistry building with him; to blow us all up."

Brade felt feverish. One was on each side of him. Each was eager to believe it suicide. Why? (An inner voice was telling him: suicide is better than murder. It's a way out; a way out. Yet, without weighing matters, without argument, without thought, he knew he wanted the truth more than a way out. In fact, truth was the only real way out. Everything else was illusion.)

Brade said, "Why suicide? What's so easy to believe about suicide? He had only half a year at the most before his doctorate."

Ranke was still the harpy. "Are you sure of that? How was his work going?"

"Very well," snapped Brade.

"How do you know?"

Brade was about to answer and saw the trap Ranke had laid for him. He had no way of avoiding it, and his silence only meant that Ranke had to take the trouble to push him into it.

Ranke said, "I suppose he told you the work was going well."

"Certainly he did," said Brade, braving it.

"How could you know he was telling the truth?"

"I have the duplicates of his records."

Ranke's smile broadened, and Foster was smiling, too. Brade became conscious of a silence in the room; of small groups suspending conversational operations and looking in his direction; of Doris, crumpling a handkerchief tightly and biting at her lower lip.

Brade knew he could convince no chemist in the room that he knew enough kinetics to judge whether Ralph's work was really going well.

Ranke's voice was honey-smooth, honey-sweet. "I know what Ralph Neufeld's original theories were and I tell you they were nonsense. I was willing to let him try the matter and prove that much to himself on the off-chance that a sidetrail might open up that would lead to something. Of course, that didn't work. It was impossible to get along with him. So he went to you and that was his real Waterloo. For a student to carry through a problem of the sort he was working on without ever consulting an expert in the field was an invitation to disaster."

That, Brade thought, must be the real thorn in the situation for Ranke. Ralph had never consulted the great man. Brade said, "You needn't excommunicate the boy's soul and consign it to hell for never having come to you for help."

"I didn't give a damn whether he came to me or not," said Ranke, lifting his chin. "Why the devil should I care? I just happen to think he was up a tree. And I tell you what, Lou. He was finally forced into recognizing the fact. He had bulled his way around and around the problem; had taken measurements and interpreted and reinterpreted them until he finally found himself with no way out. He could only tell you how well he was doing so long, and then he reached dead end. And that meant no Ph.D. So he killed himself. Why not?"

"Because," said Brade, with cold anger, "his work *was* going well. I may not be primarily a physical chemist, but I'm not altogether a plumber either. When the wind is nor'norwesterly, I can tell a Walden inversion from a photo-chemical chain reaction. I've read his reports and he was doing well."

Somehow he did not see the room as it actually was. There was a kind of blurring mist before his eyes. All the men and women who surrounded him, seemed to be facing him, with Ranke and Foster in the forefront. Behind him, there seemed a sheer drop.

Wolves! He was fighting off the wolves. The events of the previous forty-eight hours fell into strangely luminous focus. Violence had invaded the academic cloister and sent the inhabitants into a panic. They were panicking and searching for a way to propitiate the unfriendly gods. They were preparing to expiate the sin and avert retribution by sacrificing Brade.

If it were accident, it would be Brade's fault. If they were forced to accept suicide, they would do so, but would make it clear that it was Brade's inept guidance of his students that was at fault. And finally (Brade knew with a cold certainty) if the issue of murder arose, there would be only one suspect allowed. It would be expedient that one man might die for the department.

But if they thought he was going to bare his chest to the knife with nothing more than a stoical expression, they were mistaken.

He said, "You seem so certain that Ralph killed himself, Professor Ranke, that I can't help but wonder if it is perhaps an inner guilt that is driving you."

"An inner guilt?" said Ranke haughtily.

"Exactly. You threw him out of your group. You condemned him to work for what you yourself consider an inadequate sponsor. You had made it perfectly clear to him that you disapproved of his theories even in advance of experimentation" (Brade raised his voice to override the beginning of an objection from the other and cared nothing for the fact that the entire room was audience to his remarks) "and that you disliked him intensely. Perhaps Ralph felt that you would tear him and his work to shreds at his oral examinations regardless of any intrinsic value it might have. Perhaps in a moment of depression, he could not face the thought of trying to stand up to a vindictive petty tyrant with a bad case of punctured vanity."

Ranke, white-faced, croaked something incomprehensible.

Foster said, "I think we ought to leave this to the police."

But Brade wasn't through. He whirled on the other, "Or perhaps it was your C in synthetic organic that finished him."

"What are you talking about?" said Foster, with sudden uneasiness. "I had to give him what he earned."

"Was a C what he earned? I saw his final examination paper and it wasn't a C paper. I *am* an organic chemist, you'll grant me that, and you'll allow me to be a judge of a final examination paper in an organic course."

Foster blustered, "There's more than a finals involved. There was the lab work; there was his whole attitude in class—"

Brade interrupted, viciously. "It's a damned pity no one marks you on *your* attitude in class, or wonders about the satisfaction you get in picking on students who can't fight back. Someday perhaps one of them will meet you in an alley and settle a long overdue score."

Mrs. Littleby, agitated, came out to announce in a desperately soft voice, "If you please, everyone, if you please—Let's all eat now, shall we?"

Ranke and Foster fell away. Brade found himself walking through the door into the dining room in the midst of a kind of small vacuum.

And then Doris hurried over. "What happened?" she asked in a tight, breathy whisper. "How did it all start?"

Brade said through clenched teeth. "Leave it for now, Doris. I'm *glad* it happened."

He was, too. With his job gone anyway, he had nothing to lose and there was a wonderful freedom about that, a wonderful release. In what time was left him at the university, the Fosters and Rankes and all that tribe of ambitious strivers could no longer jostle him without feeling his teeth in return.

The feeling of defiance carried over. He was avoided during the buffet meal; he was left to himself. So he sought out Littleby.

"Professor Littleby."

"Ah, Brade." The department head's mechanical smile was uneasy.

"I would like to suggest, sir, that the safety lecture be made a department responsibility, since safety *is* a department responsibility. If I am to take a personal responsibility for it, as you have suggested, I want the fact reflected in a bettering of my position in the department."

He nodded curtly and walked away. He did not wait for Littleby to answer.

That also made him feel better—and cost him nothing. There was that about losing everything. No further loss is possible.

Brade and Doris left as early as they decently could.

Brade battled the traffic as though each oncoming car wore the face of Ranke and each car threatening from behind were Foster, hunching his way forward, pushing aside those who would make way, climbing over those who would not.

He said, "That's it. I'm never going to one of those things again, even if—"

He was going to finish with "even if I'm kept on." He didn't. Doris did not yet know the true position.

She said, with surprising softness, "But whatever started it?"

Brade said, "Foster warned me the police don't go for the accident theory. Neither did Foster. No chemist could believe Ralph would make that mistake accidentally. I suppose someone got in touch with the police about it."

"But why? Why should someone make trouble?"

"Some people like to make trouble. And some people might feel it their civic duty. The point is the department is willing to accept suicide and be done with it on that basis, especially if I can be made to bear the blame. The damn fools don't know what kind of a storm they're whistling up."

"But—"

"No buts. It's murder. They must know it, too, or they wouldn't be so anxious to settle for suicide. The way it happened was too complicated for suicide. He had the sodium cyanide right there. To commit suicide, all he had to do was put a few crystals in his mouth. To set up an experiment and arrange to smell hydrogen cyanide after acidification? No one would try to commit suicide by an indirect method that might possibly not work, when he had a direct and infallible method right in his hands."

His mind had made the switchover now. The danger of

unemployment was drowned out once again by the danger of an accusation of murder.

Brade slept that night, deeply and dreamlessly. The accumulated weariness of two restless nights were one reason for that, and the draining effect of the evening's excitement was another.

When he woke, he found a gray morning with a hint of rain and a definite autumn rawness in the air.

He felt gray, too. With a night between, what had seemed high battle before going to bed came to mind now as only a fishwife squabble. His own dangers had huddled in closer, and he saw no way out.

Of course, it was possible to suppose that those was backed a suicide theory most enthusiastically might be those who would have the most to fear from the alternative of murder. The most fearful of all against a possible decision in favor of murder, would be the murderer himself.

Well, did that mean that Ranke or Foster had killed Ralph? Damn it. He pushed at his bacon and eggs and thought: what motive?

Motive! The whole thing, from the very beginning, hinged on motive.

He said to Doris, "I'm going in to school today."

"Today? Sunday?"

"Just because it's Sunday. I'm getting to work on Ralph's research notebooks."

"Why?"

"You heard Ranke yesterday, didn't you? He thinks Ralph's work was going poorly and that I wouldn't know the difference."

"Would you?" said Doris, flatly.

Brade's defenses went down suddenly. "I'm not sure," he said, "but I'd better find out. And then I'd better finish up the work, too, and show those—those bastards a thing or two."

Doris said, "You know. I'm awfully afraid."

On sudden impulse, Brade rose, crossed to her side of the table and put an arm around her shoulder. "Being afraid won't help us. We've got to fight this thing out as it develops, and we will. That's all."

Her head rested against his shirt and her eyes closed. "Yes, dear," she said, and then Ginny's feet were a clatter on the steps as she came down and Doris pushed him away and called out, "You're late, Virginia, and you'll just have to eat your eggs cold."

The twin peaks of masonry on the administration building of the university rose from amidst the green of the campus as Brade turned his car out of Fifth Street and onto University Road. The building looked unnatural without heavy traffic between himself and it, without the louder noise of tires and motors, without the stronger odor of gasoline.

The university as a whole looked strange and hostile. Perhaps that was because it was Sunday, perhaps because he no longer felt they belonged to him. Something had happened the previous evening. He had severed connections. He had inwardly accepted the fact that he was no longer part of it.

His parking spot seemed hostile. There were only three others cars in sight instead of a lot-full. The chemistry building was a stranger, with the department office and the chemical museum shut when both should have been open; with his footsteps unnaturally loud in the natural Sunday silence.

He took the self-service elevator and stepped out on the fourth floor. All the doors of labs and offices were closed so that the corridor was dark. He turned on the corridor light and walked along half its length to what had been Ralph's laboratory.

He reached for his key chain and worked through the keys quickly for the one that opened the door. For a moment, he felt surprise at something he could not pin down. Oh, yes, there was one key too many.

He remembered with a pang of discomfort that the detective had brought back Ralph's key on Friday. The discomfort arose from the simultaneous thought that the same detective was not content to let matters be but suspected suicide, some sort of violence, anyway.

Somberly, Brade turned the key in the lock, opened the door, stepped in, and froze with the sudden paralysis that invariably accompanies the sight of someone where you expected to find no one.

And the other person in the laboratory, as frozen as Brade, looked up at him with startled eyes and a mouth half-open as though to scream.

14

BRADE'S muscles loosened slowly. He said in a voice that was shaken, but nevertheless under control, "Good morning, Roberta. I'm afraid you surprised me."

Roberta Goodhue put her hands in her lap. She had been turning the pages of a research notebook (and a drawer in Ralph's desk stood open) but now she let the pages flip slowly together.

She said, "Good Morning, Professor Brade."

He said, "How did you manage to get in here?"

She said, "I—I was just looking through his things. He—he was buried yesterday afternoon and I thought—I thought" (she was getting it out with difficulty) "I might find some things I could keep, something—"

She didn't finish and Brade almost completed it, by saying for her: something to remember him by.

His heart was heavy for her. What would be a good souvenir of a chemical romance between two Ph.D. students? An old test tube in which one of *his* solutions had carelessly dried? Some scattered crystals that he had weighed out, that might be put in a small envelope and pressed between the leaves of a book? A beaker to be put away in a box and sighed over?

He said, "I'm sorry I wasn't at the funeral, Roberta. I didn't know when it was to have been held." (He thought: a lousy excuse; I might have inquired.)

But Roberta said, "That's all right. There was just his mother and myself. It wasn't meant to be more than that."

Brade's mind turned back to the problem of her presence. Surely he had locked this door when he left it last. Was it possible, perhaps, that someone else had been in the lab after him and had *not* locked the door on leaving. The detective? With a duplicate key?

Oh, Lord, he was seeing detectives under every lab bench and behind every beaker now. It might have been Greg Simpson, Ralph's lab partner, who had a right to be in the lab and no compelling reason to lock the door.

But Roberta seemed to have heard his original question at last. She said in a low voice. "I have a key of my own."

"Oh? How did you get it?"

"Ralph gave it to me."

Brade said nothing for a moment. He closed the door of the laboratory and snapped the lock. He sat down on the stool near the door and looked solemnly at Roberta as she sat there on what had been Ralph's chair, in front of what had been Ralph's desk. The sun, breaking through the clouds, made its way through the not very clean window (the windows in university laboratories are rarely better than translucent) and rested upon Roberta's arm, edging the fine hairs into a ruddy color.

She isn't as bad-looking as one might think, Brade thought with some surprise. She wasn't tall or slim, to be sure, and she didn't have the Hollywood standard of good looks. Still, her eyelashes were long, her lips finely molded, the skin on her upper arm smooth and warm in coloring.

Why need it be supposed that Ralph had to be actuated by some unusual inner need to be satisfied with her? Why might there not have been a quite simple and uncomplicated sexual appeal about the affair?

He said, "I didn't know Ralph ever let anyone have a key for this door. Of course, I see that you're a logical exception."

She looked wretched.

Brade said, "Was there a reason that made it advisable for you to have a key?" He paused, and then said more kindly, "Under ordinary circumstances, this would be none of my business, but these circumstances are not ordinary."

She brushed her hair back with a quick movement of the arm and lifted her face to his. "I know what you're thinking, Professor Brade, and there's no point in lying about it. I sometimes met him here—after hours. If I had my own key I could come alone."

"For greater privacy? It would be more noticeable if you came together."

"Yes."

Brade felt embarrassment wash over him, but he shot out his next question suddenly and baldly, for the truth that might be forced out of the girl by the shock of it. He said, "Are you pregnant?"

She winced visibly and dropped her eyes. "No." (She didn't grow indignant or haughty. She simply said, no.)

"Are you sure?"

"Positive."

"Very well, Roberta. I won't say anything about this."

She said, "Thank you, Professor Brade, and I want you

to know I realize how unfair we were to you and I'm sorry for it. If we had been caught, it would have been very—sordid. And bad for you, too."

"It would have been bad for all of us," said Brade.

"It's just that we *were* going to be married and we had no place else we could really be alone. But you know about it now and if you think I had better drop out, I will. It doesn't matter much. Really."

"No," said Brade with energy. "I'm not asking you to drop out, for God's sake. As to what went on between yourself and Ralph, that's over. It's none of my business and I'm done with it. I only asked because—"

He paused momentarily. He couldn't very well tell her that for a moment he had a vision of her as a suddenly and inconveniently pregnant mistress, making herself hated by her demands for marital respectability, and resenting the betrayal that a sharp-tongued individual such as Ralph was quite capable of putting into biting and unequivocal words; resenting it to the death.

But she wasn't pregnant—or said she wasn't. Somewhere in the back of his mind the possibility lingered.

He continued lamely, "I only asked because I felt that if something, uh, unusual between the two of you had arisen, it might account for the distraction of mind that led to his accident. But now, look here, I understand how upset you must be by all this. Why don't you take a week off, or as long as you feel necessary? The lab course will do without you for that time. I'll find someone to substitute. Then, when you get through the worst of it—"

She shook her head. "Thank you, Professor Brade, but I'll keep working. It's worse when I'm in my room."

She rose and tucked her purse under her arm. She had

reached the door and was pausing a moment to unlock it when a new thought occurred to Brade.

He said, "Roberta. Wait."

She waited, not turning to look at him. Brade paused, too, feeling the complete fool and wondering how to put the question.

He said, "I hope you won't mind my asking a very personal question."

"More personal than those you've already asked, Professor Brade?"

Brade cleared his throat. "Maybe, in a way. I have my reasons for asking, though. Well, it amounts to this. Have you ever had any trouble with Professor Foster?"

She turned now. "Trouble, Professor Brade?" Her voice took on a rising note and her eyebrows lifted.

Brade thought disgustedly: Oh, hell, *say* it.

He said, "To put it bluntly, has Professor Foster ever made a pass at you?"

Roberta said, "The question is scarcely personal. Professor Foster makes no secret about his passes. Yes, I've had my share. No more than any girl here endures, but no fewer, either. Professor Foster is very kind-hearted and distributes himself freely and equally."

"Did Ralph know about it?"

She stiffened again. "Why do you ask that?"

"Because I think Ralph did know, didn't he?"

The girl was silent.

Brade said, "Since Foster isn't particularly secret about the remarks he makes" (and perhaps a little more than remarks, he thought; "Handies" Foster) "Ralph would know and he would undoubtedly resent it and make the resentment known to Professor Foster."

Roberta said angrily, "No one pays any attention to

Professor Foster. He's tiresome sometimes, but it doesn't mean anything. If any girl responded in the least, he'd jump out a window to get away."

"But the point is, Ralph *did* pay attention to it and he let Professor Foster know."

"I think I'll go now, Professor. I'm—not well." She turned to the door again, then turned back and said with a sudden wistfulness. "I wonder— Will you be needing Ralph's research notebooks?"

Brade said, "For a while. Eventually, I think I can let you have them."

She hesitated almost as though she wanted to say something else. But she didn't. She left.

Five minutes later, Brade could see her through the lab window, walking out the main door of the chemistry building, then crossing the bricked pavement, then down the stone pathway and across the campus.

She had evaded his final questions, of course, and the evasion equalled an affirmative.

Of course! Ralph would *have* to be jealous, would *have* to fear desperately the loss of anything he owned. He would be just the one to fire up at those same little tricks of Foster's that all others took in bored stride.

And he was the type who would steamingly confront Foster, demand that it stop, threaten to take the matter to higher authorities. And that was a deadly threat.

The administration could blink at Foster's ways as long as no one minded, as long as there was no stink about it. But once a stink did arise, there would be a difference. A fatal difference.

After all, a professor might drink himself into a stupor every night; might bumble out lectures no one could understand; might bathe only during Lent; might be unbearably rude; intolerably boring; intensively obnoxious; and all would be forgiven. With tenure, he would be immovable despite all that.

But two levers could always remove him, tenure or not. One was disloyalty (a comparatively modern crime) and the other was as old as Abelard, for it was moral turpitude. And Foster skated the edge of that constantly. An actual complaint would push him over the edge.

With the complaint actually in prospect, would that explain murder? Would murder be the way to get rid of the prospective complainant?

Or did that only explain a C?

After all, this gave Foster a possible motive, but it didn't improve the matter of opportunity. How would Foster know the way in which Ralph conducted his experiments. How would he know that Erlenmeyer flasks containing sodium acetate would be waiting for him in the cabinet?

He shrugged his shoulders and turned to Ralph's research notebooks. There were five of them, numbered neatly, and Brade opened one at random.

He had the duplicates in his own office, but if Ralph had been like every other grad student Brade had ever known, he would have scrap work and comments on the back of the white-sheet originals that might come in handy.

He flicked through the pages and thought that there was no question that Ralph was the ideal notebook-keeper. He was clear, concise and almost painfully precise. Brade had seen the ancient notebooks in which Cap Anson's crabbed handwriting had recorded *his* Ph.D.

work but even that model of thoroughness was exceeded by Ralph.

Surely, Brade thought, he could follow this. Ralph explained his work as though assuming none but elementary knowledge on the part of whoever read it. (Guiltily, he thought, maybe Ralph was writing this for me and assuming what in his opinion is so.) Damn it, then, he *would* understand it. He just had to be less frightened of the mathematics.

Well, then, let's be systematic. Let's start right now.

He turned to Notebook One. The first pages were given over to Ralph Neufeld's work under Ranke; a listing of the papers he had read in advance of beginning actual research; summaries of their comments; his own comments and theories. It was all very neat and superlatively organized. Brade remembered going over this once before, a year and a half ago, when he had first accepted Ralph as a student.

With his experience of Ralph since, he was suddenly astonished that so little of Ralph's instability seemed to lap over into his work. His notes were completely objective.

Brade found comments such as: "Professor Ranke points out an inconsistency in the concept that—" or "Professor Ranke seems unconvinced that—" Yet the comments never descended to passion. They were cold.

Even the end of the Ranke period was marked by the mere statement: "Today was my last as a student of Professor O. Ranke." No mention of the fight with the other student; no expression of self-defense or of rancor. That one sentence and nothing more on that page.

The date that followed was more than a month later

and the new page began: "Today was my first as a student of Professor L. Brade."

The pages that followed were familiar to him. At the beginning of Ralph's studies under him, the sheets had been handed in weekly and explained page by page. Later, they had been handed in more and more irregularly and explained more and more sketchily; finally not explained at all. Had Ralph grown discouraged at Brade's inability to understand it all properly? Was that why Ralph had hated Brade? (But Charlie Emmett thought it was fear, not hate.)

Brade bit his lower lip and paused to consider lunch. He shook his head. The sandwich shop in the building was closed on Sunday; he had brought nothing from home; the nearest decent restaurant was a ten-minute brisk walk away.

He decided to do without lunch and returned to the books.

Ralph had been particularly thorough in his description of individual experiments. Each experiment was preceded by the reason for its performance and was followed by an interpretation. Where the results seemed off base, Ralph included his theories and speculations as to what had gone wrong.

It was helpful. It was more than helpful and Brade's spirits began to rise. The mathematics was rough, but at least no steps were omitted.

If Ralph had a flaw as a research chemist, Brade decided, it was that he seemed a bit too attached to his preconceived theories. That is, any experiment that seemed to back up a thought he had had was allowed to stand without rechecking. Experiments that went counter to his theories were checked and rechecked and, sometimes, explained away.

There were a great many experiments that went counter-theory through volumes one and two and a certain pettishness began to creep into Ralph's comments. Remarks like: "Must improve temperature control. See Brade about decent thermostat if work is to have any meaning at all."

It was the omission of the otherwise meticulously inserted "Professor" that seemed most indicative of snapping temper to Brade. (And hate?) Yet the man had controlled himself under much more intensive conditions when working with Ranke. Was it because Ranke, even when he disagreed with Brade, was a mainstay, a rock to fall back on; whereas Brade was—nothing?

It was about here that duplicates began to be handed in infrequently and in large batches and Brade no longer recognized the pages or remembered them even dimly. (He was much to blame for this. He felt bitterly ashamed and swore, silently, that no student in the future would do research without him.)

About the beginning of the third book, things broke for the better quite suddenly. For one thing, Ralph developed the line of experimentation which thereafter proved fruitful and—

Brade gasped in sudden surprise as he turned a page. Ralph described the method of experimentation carefully and in full, including the preparation in advance of the sodium acetate aliquots in ten flasks. It gave Brade an odd feeling, a kind of prickling in the spine, to think that any halfway competent chemist finding this particular page would know exactly how to poison Ralph as he had been poisoned.

But he forbore to speculate. To hell with murder and murderers. At the moment, he had to estimate his own chances at being able to carry on the research.

The experiments continued well. The graphs on log-log paper showed points that fell beautifully along a straight line. Brade was relieved. His backing of Ralph's work last evening to Ranke had been a good part bluff, but here were the graph, the equations, everything from A to Z. Anyone could check them and see for himself that Ralph's work was going well, that his theories were working out.

Even Ranke could.

Brade stopped to look at some scrap calculations on the back of the sheets. They had been erased.

Brade frowned. Theoretically, there were supposed to be no erasures in the notebooks. Anything wrong, anything in error, must only be crossed out lightly, so that it might not stay to mislead and yet might remain legible for future reference. (Even mistakes can be useful.)

Of course, the erasure on the back of a sheet was venial. The back of a sheet was not really part of the notebook. He studied the figures more closely and his frown deepened. He thought a bit, turned a few more pages and came across other erasures.

For a long time, then, he sat in the chair without looking at the books, while the afternoon hours lengthened.

It didn't seem possible. In his entire experience as a research chemist, he had never come across a case before. And yet—there seemed no doubt.

No doubt! Brade had discovered that Charlie Emmett

was right. Ralph must have feared Brade with a most deadly fear and Brade knew why, now, and was sick with the knowledge.

15

IT took a while for all the meaning to seep into Brade and the multiplicity of the hurts numbed him.

To follow up Ralph's work was impossible now. There would be no startling paper, no unusual contribution, nothing with which to dazzle the department and the outside chemical world. Cap Anson had been right. Otto Ranke had been right. He himself had been wrong.

The knocking at the door was repeated three times before he heard it. When he finally cried, "Come in," nothing much happened except for a futile rattling of the knob.

Brade rose to unlock the door. It was as though someone else's muscles were moving. He did not even have room in his mind to wonder who might be at the door on a Sunday; nor room to be astonished to find it was Plainclothesman Jack Doheny, wearing the same dark blue suit with the thin white lines he had worn Thursday night when they had first met over Ralph Neufeld's dead body.

Doheny looked about casually and said, "I hope you don't mind talking to me a while, Professor."

"If you wish," said Brade without much feeling about it at that shattered moment.

"I called at your home but your wife said you were over here. So I came around." He looked around again. "Mind if I smoke, Prof?"

"Go ahead."

Doheny lit a cigar carefully and sat down in a chair in response to Brade's silent invitation. He pulled an ashtray toward himself and said, "Looks like both of us are putting in a bit of Sunday work."

Brade said, "Are you here to ask questions about Ralph Neufeld, or is it something else I can help you with?"

"It's the boy all right, Professor. I can't seem to get it out of my mind. Funny. It just wasn't right from the very beginning."

"How wasn't it right from the very beginning?" asked Brade, cautiously.

"Well, you know, Prof, I don't know a thing about chemistry. Nothing. So I felt pretty lost the first time I was here. Still, I been in my business so long I can't help but get the feel of something wrong when I'm telling myself: watch out, Jack, you're out of your league."

"I don't understand you."

"It ain't easy to explain. Lookit, Professor, take you. Say you got a new kind of chemical in a test tube and you're wondering what can it do? I'll bet you can make a kind of guess even before you do anything to it, before you test it. You tell yourself, this looks like the kind that'll explode. Or, watch out for this one, now, it's a poisonous one; or this one will turn black if I add some of this here stuff to it."

Brade said, "Certainly, if I knew the structural formula of a new compound, I could make certain deductions about its properties."

"And you'd be right pretty near every time, huh?"

"I'd be often right, I suppose."

"Sure. It comes with experience. A kind of feel for things maybe you can't even explain sometimes."

"Perhaps so," said Brade, doubtfully.

"All right, Professor. Now I spent twenty-five years working with human beings, like you been working with chemicals. I've got an education about people like you can't get in school. I can spot something wrong about a person like you can see something funny in a chemical. Sometimes I'm on the wrong track like you could be sometimes with chemicals, but mostly I'm right, like mostly you are."

Brade felt his apprehension growing, yet kept enough self-possession to see that all this might be designed precisely to cause his apprehension to grow and nothing more. He said, flatly, "What are you getting at?"

"What I'm trying to say is that when I talked with you Thursday, there was something wrong about you."

"There certainly was. I'd never in my life seen a dead body before and this one was one of my students. I wasn't myself."

"That so? I can see that, Prof. Honest. But lookit." Doheny worked at his cigar slowly, with methodical puffings, turning it to make sure it burned evenly. "Chemistry's a lot like cooking, see. You got ingredients. You mix them and heat them or do whatever the hell (excuse me) you do to them. Chemistry is maybe more complicated, but if you think of a cook in a kitchen, you got a picture of a chemist in a laboratory.

"Now suppose a cook is making a cake. She needs flour, milk, eggs, vanilla, bicarb, God know what. She gets 'em all down on the counter and starts adding and mixing and whatnot. But after she uses 'em, she leaves the boxes and bottles on the counter. Maybe she puts the milk back in the refrigerator, but chances are she won't budge the flour or vanilla, say. What she *don't* do, is go to the pantry to get flour, pour out some, take the flour back to the pantry, get milk, add some, take the milk back to the refrigerator, get flavoring and so on. Get it?"

"I get it, Mr. Doheny. But what is the application to this case?"

"Well, your boy was mixing his kind of cake, and he was adding," (Doheny cast a quick glance at a little card he withdrew from his shirt pocket), "sodium acetate, only he got sodium cyanide instead. So why wasn't the bottle of cyanide on the workspace near him? Why was it back on the shelf?"

"What's the difference where it was?" (Brade knew the difference, but the question was, what did this suddenly formidable man with the round, unintelligent face think the difference was?)

"Maybe," said Doheny, judiciously. "It means nothing. Maybe, for instance, it was on the desk near him and you put it back on the shelf automatically when you found the body. You know—without thinking. Did you?"

Brade smelled a trap. He dared not tell a lie. He said, "No."

"Or maybe the kid was the kind of character who did crazy things. Maybe he poured out some powder and walked fifteen feet to put the bottle back before going on.

Except that I noticed he had an empty little jug behind all the glassware he was working with, and the jug, or flask, or whatever, had a bit of powder in it, so he was the kind who let things stay a while. So it seemed funny, then."

Brade's thin lips remained pressed together. He said nothing.

Doheny said, "So I worried about it. I took the bottle of poison from the shelf to where the boy'd been working and went through some motions and asked: Hey, Prof, anything funny about this? I thought I'd check and see if you got that same funny thing. I figured sure you'd say: hey, how come the bottle is on the shelf instead of where he was working? Only you didn't, Prof. You just looked blank. And then I said to myself: Jack, something's funny with the prof. He's too smart to be this dumb! See what I mean? You and chemicals; me and people."

Brade said angrily, "Damn it, I was upset, I wasn't thinking clearly."

"I'll say you weren't, Prof. The thing was funny enough so I thought I'd just ask around a bit before knocking off. And you know what? Some people said to me that this acetate stuff felt different from cyanide when you stuck a spoon into it. That so, Professor?"

Again Brade hesitated, and again he saw no safety in a lie. He said, "In a way, it does."

"Then some people said this kid, Ralph, was such a careful worker they didn't see how he could make such a mistake. He always double-checked, seems like. That right, Professor?"

"He was a careful worker."

"Well, you know, Professor," the genial smile did not leave Doheny's ruddy face, "you were so upset, you didn't say either of those things? You never once said the kid wasn't likely to mistake the bottles for this reason or that? What's more, you've had over two days since to cool down in and still you never called me to say: hey, I thought of something I forgot to tell you. So maybe my first funny feeling about you has something to it."

"Not much," said Brade, with sudden anger, "except that I'm not bright about these things. I'm not a detective. That's all."

Doneny nodded. "Yeah. I admit it ain't much—all by itself. But lookit, again. Maybe you were all upset and like that, but still and all, you were right there asking for the kid's key to this laboratory. Remember that."

"Yes, I do."

"All right, why'd you ask? You could of called the next day or come down to the station to pick it up or let us keep it, since you probably got one of your own. But you asked for it. Now why?"

Brade was outraged. "I just happened to think of it. There was nothing more to it than that. I just happened to think of it." (My God, thought Brade, helplessly, that was all there was to it. What am I getting into here?)

Doheny held up a plump hand. "Sure, sure. Maybe that explains it. I ain't saying it don't. Still I thought: what about another explanation? That's my job, you know, to think of other explanations. Maybe you were pretty anxious no one should come into the lab without you knowing it. Maybe it made you nervous having the police hold the key." The ash on his cigar had grown long. He tapped it gently into the ashtray. "I just wondered."

Brade realized he had made a mistake skipping lunch. The emptiness in his stomach and the odor of the cigar smoke combined to give him an edge of illness and dull his thought. He said, "I assure you I had no such motive."

"But I thought I'd check, Prof. There was just enough funny about you, so that after I left, I hung about outside. The light went on in the kid's laboratory and stayed on for quite a while. You left a good hour after I did. So I had the boys bring back the kid's key and I went in the lab again and, you know, you'd been working in it. There were some chemicals standing around that weren't there before and some little jugs of powder."

Brade cleared his throat with difficulty.

Doheny said, "So I asked one of our own chemists to come over. We got chemists on the force, too, Prof. He looked the place over and he said it was possible you were testing for cyanide and he took some of the stuff in the little jugs back to the police lab and he says they were acetate. So—what were you doing in the lab, Professor?"

Brade saw no way out of it. In a low, steady voice, he told Doheny what he had done in Ralph's laboratory on Thursday evening, of the one cyanide flask and its acetate sisters, of Ralph's method of working.

"And you didn't tell us?" said Doheny.

"I'm afraid not."

"Afraid you were going to be all tangled up in a murder rap?"

"If you mean I thought suspicion of murder might rest on me, you're right."

"Well, you did the wrong thing about it. This would make the suspicion stronger to a jury."

"Why?" said Brade, heatedly. "If I were the murderer, I wouldn't have to check those flasks. I'd know."

"If you weren't the murderer, why were you keeping secrets? That's what the jury would wonder. Now, once you start out not being open and aboveboard, they start wondering what the hell did you *really* do in the lab. Maybe you ain't telling the truth, now."

"I swear to you—"

"You don't have to swear to me. Save that for the courtroom if it ever comes to that." He tapped his cigar again and said, "Point is, you thought it was murder from the very first."

"Murder or suicide."

"Suicide?"

"*You* thought it might be suicide. At least the word has gone round that you were asking questions as to Ralph's state of mind before his death."

"Now who told you that, I wonder."

"Does it matter?"

"No. Just wondered if you'd tell me. Sure, I asked questions to cover the suicide angle, but I didn't believe in it very much. A suicide usually leaves notes."

"There is no law that they must."

"Sure thing. But *usually*. Point is, a suicide generally feels sorry for himself, you know. He figures that once he's dead, all the people who were mean to him would feel pretty bad and think maybe if they had a chance to do it all over again, they would be nice to him. It sort of keeps his spirits up, thinking of this while he's getting ready to knock himself off. You know, thinking of how lousy other people will feel. So generally, he leaves a note to whoever he wants to make sure will feel particularly lousy, usually to his mother or his wife.

"Now when a suicide don't leave a note, it means he's pretty sure the right people will suffer without his help. They ain't generally that confident, and I, personally, ain't ever come across a suicide without a note or some sort of message yet.

"In the case of this kid, he not only left no note but, if he was really a suicide, he went to a lot of trouble to make it look like an accident. Don't you think so, Professor?"

Brade was willing to agree to that. "Yes, I do."

"Sometimes suicides do that. Question of insurance, but the kid got no insurance. Question of family disgrace on account of religion, but the kid just got a mother and neither one's much on religion. I tried other angles which didn't work. There was just no sense in a suicide being made to look like accident. But there's a lot of sense in making a homicide look like an accident. So someone else substituted the cyanide."

"But who?" asked Brade.

"I dunno for sure," said Doheny. "Maybe you did."

"But I had no reason to." Brade's mind had been numbed into a kind of anesthesia. He could talk about this without pain.

"On the other hand, maybe you did have reason, Prof. I picked up some notions asking about the way I did. For instance, I got one notion that you're not doing so well around the college, here; that maybe you're on the skids. I ain't saying it's so; but some people made a few strong hints in that direction. Also, this boy, Ralph, didn't get alone with you. Now if your own student goes around saying you're nothing much, it might just give you the little extra push to put you out of a job. Maybe there's reason there for you to see his mouth was shut—permanently."

Brade felt distinctly revolted. It was something too ridiculous to argue about. He said, "Just the same, Mr. Doheny, I have come across something now, that makes suicide very logical and gives us a good reason for Ralph having tried to make it appear accidental." (Why not, he thought. It could be this way, at that.)

"That so? Suppose you tell me." Doheny did not sound impressed.

"I intend to." Brade stared sadly down at the research notebooks. He had told Ranke the evening before that he was enough of a physical chemist to be able to tell that Ralph's work was going well. He was talking in the heat of fury, but he might have upheld that boast. At least, he could understand the results deduced from Ralph's data and see how they fitted Ralph's theories. One thing, however, he had taken on faith; one thing was always taken on faith—the integrity of the investigator.

Brade said, "Ralph Neufeld had certain theories that he was trying to prove or disprove by certain experiments. If he succeeded in proving his theories, he would make a name for himself and probably get a good job. If he did not prove his theories, he might not even get his degree. Do you see that?"

"Sure."

"Now this morning I've been going over his research notebooks and I find that at first his work went poorly. He grew more and more anxious until finally he took steps to make *sure* his theories worked. He began to falsify his observations. He deliberately adjusted his measurements to make them fit his theories."

Doheny said, "Like a bank employee going crooked and fixing the books to cover up."

"Yes. Exactly like that."

Doheny paused and gave the matter a deal of thought. He said, "Would you swear to this in court, Professor?"

Brade thought of what he had found in the books, the

sudden change to successful experiments, the erased data. He thought of little things like Simpson's story of Ralph's fury when his lab partner had approached too closely when Ralph was writing up data. He said, "I think I would. But you do see, don't you? To the very end, he went faithfully through the experiments as though something inside him forced him to be the pretense of an honest scientist even though he wasn't one any longer. It was a terrible, terrible thing he was doing, and finally he could stand his own disgrace no longer. He killed himself."

"But why should he make it look like an accident?"

"Because if it were suicide, people would wonder why. They might look through his books, find his disgrace. If it were an accident, no one would look for motives. His memory would remain clear."

"He could have destroyed his books."

"I have duplicates."

"Wouldn't he figure you'd continue this work and find out, anyway?"

"Perhaps not," said Brade, in a low voice. "He thought little of my ability to follow this kind of work. Perhaps he thought I would simply abandon the project once he was gone. Do you see, Mr. Doheny? Do you see how suicide fits now?"

Doheny put his hand to his chin and rubbed hard. He said, "I see how it fits, Professor, but not suicide. What you tell me now could be your funeral. It gives you a better motive for murder than any I ever figured."

16

BRADE stared in pure dismay. "Are you dismissing suicide that easily? I've explained why there would be no note. Or perhaps you don't understand what an enormous crime the falsification of experimental data is to a scientist?"

Doheny seemed impervious to Brade's hard glare. He held out his right hand. "Say, can I take a look at one of those books?"

Brade handed him one and Doheny leafed through it soberly. He shook his head. "Just means nothing to me. But you can look through this and see there's something wrong with the figures?"

"Of course I can," said Brade.

"Well, you got the experience for it. And I got the experience to tell when something's wrong with suicide. Lookit, Prof, in my experience there are two kinds of people who get involved in violence. One kind is the kind that hates themselves. They're no good, they figure. Nothing that happens to them is any good. They got nothing on the ball. If something bad happens, and everything that happens *is* bad, it's their own fault."

"You can go up to a guy like that and kick him in the

butt for no reason at all, and they won't get mad at you. They'll figure they got a kickable butt and it's their own fault they got kicked. Sometimes these guys feel good, maybe even hilarious; but that's only temporary. They slip back into the blues."

Brade said, "Manic-depressives."

"That what you call them?" said Doheny. "Anyway, these guys can end up violently. They're the ones that are suicide bait. With them, you got to hide the knives and ropes, or you're done. Now on the other side, you got another kind of guy. Say, this shop-talk ain't boring you, I hope." He stubbed out his cigar. "I get carried away. Maybe you're not interested."

"Please go on. I'm obviously intimately concerned with the matter."

"All right, then. You got this other kind, the kind of people who hate the whole world. Not themselves, you understand, just everybody else. Nothing can happen but what it's someone else's fault. A guy like that can do the damndest jackass thing, and he'll be sure it was because someone else sneezed a block away. He could kick *you* in the butt, then go to the police about it because you had a book in your hip pocket and he hurt his toe. What's more, he's sure everybody's got it in for him; they're plotting against him; they're all set to rip him up."

"Paranoid," said Brade.

"Okay. Give it a name. Now the dead kid was this second kind of guy. Right?"

Brade said, slowly, "I suppose he was."

"Sure he was. Now that kind of guy never kills himself because nothing's ever his fault. You, Prof, might kill yourself if you doctored the books and got overcome with shame. This kid wouldn't though. He wouldn't blame himself. He'd know for sure it was someone else's fault; he'd been forced into it, see. He would say he was just doing it to protect himself; or maybe to save humanity. No matter what, this kind of guy doesn't kill himself; he kills someone else—or he gets killed."

Brade swallowed uncomfortably, for Doheny, bereft of proper terminology, seemed, nevertheless, to be making sense.

Doheny said, "Now forget suicide and follow this thing through. Supposing the boy hadn't got himself killed. Suppose he had finished this stuff here. What would have happened?"

Brade said, "He might have been trapped by Professor Ranke at his doctor's orals—at his examination, that is."

"And suppose this professor didn't catch him?"

"Well, it's likely Ranke wouldn't. No one would think of questioning his observations. So he'd get his degree and published a paper. Eventually, though, when other experimenters tried to confirm his results, it would turn out that he was all wrong."

"Could they tell he faked?"

"He'd be so wrong, there might be suspicions to that effect."

"And what would that do for you, Prof?"

"It wouldn't do me any good," muttered Brade. Why try to deny that?

"It could do you a lot of harm, maybe."

"Well, yes."

"Maybe some people might think you helped along with the fakery. That possible?"

"I doubt anyone would ever think *that*," said Brade, indignantly, but he thought of Ranke's spleen and of what it was capable.

Doheny watched the other calmly. "Or maybe they'd just say the boy pulled his tricks under your nose because you were too dumb to catch on and the kid knew it."

Brade flushed and made an inarticulate sound.

The detective said, "So if you found out about the fakery last month, say, instead of today—"

"I found out today," said Brade.

"I'm not saying you didn't. I'm just making an if. *If* you found out last month, you'd have to stop this thing somehow and you couldn't just expose the boy, could you? That would still leave you looking pretty dumb. Maybe the only way out for you was to arrange an accident for the boy, get rid of his books, and bury the whole thing."

Brade said, "Until today, I have every intention of continuing his work. I have witnesses to that."

"You have witnesses, maybe, who heard you *say* that. But are you going to continue his work?"

"I can't, now."

"And if I hadn't come in here, today, would you have told anyone the real reason why you weren't continuing it?"

Brade's lips compressed.

Doheny said, "You see what I mean about having a darned good motive. It's only your word you just found out the faking today."

Brade said, angrily, "Are you arresting me?"

"No."

"Why not, if I have such a good motive?"

Doheny smiled. "I ain't satisfied you did it yet, Prof. I'm still playing the field. But the fact is you're in a hole, so you better help me, if you want to get out of it. F'instance, if you didn't do it, who did?"

"I don't know."

"No suspicions? Nobody with some kind of motive?"

"Well—I have no real reasons to suspect anyone and just to throw names around would be unfair and—and cowardly."

Doheny stirred in his seat. "You're an unusual guy, Professor. Generally, people don't mind saying nasty things about other people. All they need is an excuse so they can be rats without feeling like rats. Know what I mean? If they can tell themselves they are only helping to solve a terrible crime, that excuses them. How come you're different?"

Brade said, "Will trying to spread suspicion help me? Or harm me?"

Doheny's smile broadened. "You know, Prof, I got the idea you don't trust me. Well, let's look for possible suspects. This was a carefully planned murder, so we can cut out self-defense or impulse. Now what makes a guy go through with murder in the first degree. It could be fear. Like if it was you, maybe. You'd be afraid of what would happen to your reputation if those crooked books came out. Or it could be greed, only the kid didn't have a cent and nobody makes any money out of him being dead except maybe the undertaker. Or it could be love or hate, which are about the same as each other as far as murder is concerned. Well, now, it seems there's a girl here called Jean Makris was thrown over by this Ralph, and she's taking it hard."

Brade was surprised. "Who told you that?"

"A couple of people, Professor. I told you. Give a person the idea he's being noble and you'll be surprised how much dirt he'll spill, and like it, too. Now this Jean

Makris, would she have the know-how to handle chemicals? She's just a secretary, right?"

"She might have the know-how," said Brade, reluctantly (was he trying to save himself by deliberately blackening another person, as Doheny obviously expected him to do as a matter of course?). "A secretary at a university picks up a good deal of rule-of-thumb knowledge concerning the material she works with daily. She would know about cyanide, I should judge."

"Well, that's a thing to keep in mind. And we don't have to worry about alibis, because the substitution of cyanide could have been done any time over a period of days."

"Yes."

"Then there's another girl who's having a romance with him. One of your girls, in fact."

"My only girl student. I found that out day before yesterday."

"Not before, Prof? They were keeping it a secret?"

"Apparently there was some question as to whether the boy's mother would approve."

Doheny chuckled. "That shows kids don't know everything. The mother knew about it. She was the one who told me. She said when a girl visits a boy to talk chemistry, maybe it's chemistry. But when she visits once or twice a week to talk chemistry, it ain't chemistry."

Brade said, hesitantly, "Love isn't usually a murder motive, unless there's been a—falling-out."

Doheny said, "First thing I thought, too. The mother says no. She says the day before it happened, they were together and getting along real nice. I checked on that, though. For instance, they used to sit at a neighborhood ice cream store for sundaes or sodas. The soda jerk knew them. He says about a week before the murder they were in the store and a big fight was going on between them in whispers."

"Ah," said Brade, with sudden leaping interest.

"That sounds good, huh? But it was only about what kind of a sundae to have." The detective smiled. "The guy behind the counter says he thinks Ralph was telling the girl to lay off the rich desserts."

"She *is* somewhat overweight," said Brade.

"Well, she won out, though. The clerk said she kept holding out for fudge real excited-like, and she ended with a chocolate fudge sundae. He remembers, because he went light on the whipcream, so she wouldn't hate herself too much in the morning. Do you get the point of this?

"*Is* there a point to this?"

"Sure! When a young couple get all hot and bothered about what kind of ice cream to have, you can bet they're not getting set to break off. If he were ditching her (which is what it would have to be if she's the one who killed him) he wouldn't give a damn if she were tucking away a few calories. So I figure the old lady was right and they weren't breaking off."

"Sounds thin to me," said Brade. "Ralph might have just been using any excuse to start fights and get rid of her."

"Oh, it ain't jury evidence," Doheny agreed at once, "and I ain't crossed her off all the way. Now, what else you think we got, Professor?"

Brade could endure it no longer. He burst out with sudden truculence, "This won't help you, Officer."

"What?"

"I know why you've come and I'm not quite the fool you think I am. You've got speculations about me but none of what you call jury evidence. You think that by making out in friendly fashion, by assuming an appearance of frankness, you can diddle me into making some bad slips."

"You mean like telling me the books were faked."

Brade reddened slowly. "Yes. Like that. Only it was the truth, and I honestly thought it pointed to suicide. Maybe it doesn't. But you can't get anything out of me that will prove my guilt, because I'm not guilty. I don't mind your thinking I'm guilty; that's your job. I do mind your trying to get the proof of guilt out of me in this behind-the-back sort of way."

Suddenly, there was a look of complete gravity on the detective's plump face. He said, "Professor, don't get me wrong. I could be trying to fool you, sure. That's part of my job, too. Fact is, though, I ain't. I'm on your side, and I'll tell you why, too.

"If you did this, Prof, you killed a young kid to save your own reputation for brains. It takes a special kind of guy to do that—a brain-proud guy, if you know what I mean. A guy who thinks nothing must stand in the way of other people knowing how smart he is, even if he was to tell them himself; even if he has to kick them in the face with it and smear ignorance all over them.

"Now, Professor, I spoke to you Thursday night. I was talking to a chemist, you, and I didn't know anything about chemistry. You had to explain a lot of stuff to me, and you did it without making me feel like I was a criminal or a moron not to know offhand what it took you twenty years to learn. A guy who can talk to a dope like me and not feel it necessary to make me feel dumb isn't the kind of guy who would kill someone just so people wouldn't know he wasn't perfectly smart."

Brade said, "Thank you."

"And I like you for it, too. The only thing is," he rose and gravely moved toward the door, "that me and people is like you and chemicals. I'm right mostly but sometimes I'm wrong. Well, I won't bother you anymore for now." He lifted a hand in farewell and left, leaving Brade to stare after him thoughtfully.

His silent preoccupation lasted through dinner which went off in almost a complete silence. Even Ginny was subdued and was sent off to bed in what was almost a whisper.

It was only afterward, with the Sunday night drama low-voiced on television and with Brade watching it without really seeing it that Doris sat down opposite him and said, "Did anything happen today that you care to tell me about?"

Brade looked up at her slowly. She was a little paler than usual, but seemed calm. A free corner of his mind was surprised, had been since last night, that she had said nothing about the set-to at the Littleby's. He had expected her, somehow, to be wild at his folly, to blame him bitterly for his rashness in brawling before Littleby's eyes at Littleby's home.

But she had not and even now she did not.

Clearly, then, and with no attempt to palliate, Brade told her the events of the day, beginning with Roberta's disclosures, continuing on through Ralph's notebooks, and ending with the conversation with Doheny.

Through it all, she did not say one word.

And when he had done, she asked only, "What will you do now, Lou?"

"Find out who did it—somehow."

"Do you think you can?"

"I must."

She said, "You predicted all this Thursday night, and I made it harder for you by my anger. And now I'm very afraid, Lou."

And somehow because she just sat there, very afraid, he was overcome with tenderness and almost ran to her, sinking to his knees by her chair. "Why, Doris, why? I didn't really do it, you know."

"I know that." Her voice was muffled and indistinct. She didn't look at him. "But what if they think you did?"

He said, "They won't. I'm not afraid of that."

It struck him with sudden force that he was not merely consoling her. The fear that had been so sharp and saturating three nights ago had dulled almost to the vanishing point, though the danger of the situation had grown so much worse.

Because the danger had grown so much worse, there was a queer kind of perversity about it. The near-certainty of losing his job had relieved him by removing his chronic fear of losing it; the actuality of suspicion of murder had relieved him by removing the chronic fear of being suspected.

He said, "This is something we'll have to live through, Doris, and we will. Don't cry. Please don't cry."

He put his hand under her chin and lifted her head. "You won't help me at all by crying."

Doris blinked her eyes and smiled weakly. "The detective seems a rather nice man," she said.

"He's not what I've imagined detectives to be like, certainly, and he makes a deal of sense sometimes. The funny thing is his good sense always catches me by surprise because to me he looks like the comic policeman in a movie."

Doris said, "Shall I make a drink for both of us? Just a little one?"

"All right."

She came back with the two drinks and said calmly, "I've been thinking about what the detective said concerning the type of man who could have killed Ralph; one who was brain-proud. Isn't that what he said?"

"Yes, and it's a good phrase. I'll have to remember it."

"Doesn't that fit Otto Ranke?"

Brade nodded somberly. "It does. But that doesn't matter in his case. Ranke had no reputation to lose in Ralph's crookedness. Quite the contrary. He had more or less committed himself to Ralph's being wrong. The last thing he'd want to do would be to hide Ralph's fakery. No, dear, only *my* reputation was at stake."

Doris said, in a small voice, "But who else then?"

Brade held his glass immovably in his hand and stared at it. "Well, you know, I've been sitting here and I'm wondering about one little point. If what Doheny told me was accurate, word for word, then I think I'm beginning to have an idea. One word he used could have a double meaning, and I don't think Doheny realized that. I honestly don't. One word!"

17

DORIS said hopefully, "What is it?"

For a moment, Brade looked at her without seeing her, then he said, softly, "Probably nothing and not worth talking about. I'll have to think about it a bit more. And meanwhile, Doris, let's go to bed early and say to hell with it and get some sleep." He slipped his arm about her shoulders, pressing her gently to himself.

She nodded. "You have to lecture tomorrow, you know."

"I have to lecture every day. Don't let that worry you."

"All right, then. Just let me put the dishes in the washer and then we'll go to bed."

"Good. And, Doris, don't worry. Leave things to me."

She smiled at him.

He thought of the smile as he lay in bed, staring at the night-blackness, feeling the clean coolness of a new pillowcase. He could feel Doris stirring very gently next to him with the slow movement of one who was not asleep and was anxious not to disturb a bed partner who might be.

Her smile had been a warm one, a comforting one, and he wondered where it came from?

—Brain-proud man! (His thoughts had made an erratic jump.) That was Otto Ranke, all right. But why? His reputation was fixed. Everyone knew he was a brilliant man. Then why was he so ostentatiously brain-proud?

Was he proud of his brain or ashamed of it? Was it a kind of insecurity, a basic lack of belief in his own intelligence, that forced him to display it constantly and preen it and over-bear anyone who might threaten his position?

Insecurity!

And Foster? Pushing. Advancing. With a young, pretty wife who accepted him for what he was. Where was his need to prove over and over again to everything female that came his way that he was a man of sexual prowess? And to every male that he was a man of wit, even when it was the poor one-sided contest of teacher and student?

Even poor Cap! With a completed and successful career, he yet doubted the position of his name and memory with respect to posterity and struggled to produce a book that would preserve both. Poor Cap and the longing way he had spoken of Berzelius' baronetcy—

Brade bit his lips. They were all suffering from the universal disease. Insecurity!

You popped out into the world and the womb was gone. It was cold now and the light hurt. You had to work to breathe and work to eat. All the comforts and warmth and darkness and cuddle were gone, gone, gone. And you were never secure again.

He moved suddenly. "Doris!" He breathed it, half afraid she was asleep and that he would waken her.

But her voice answered at once, a little blurred and drowsy, but answering, "Yes, Lou?"

"You don't seem as—upset—as I thought you would be." (He meant about Saturday night at Littleby's place, yet could not quite bring himself to be specific.)

She said, softly, "You're taking care of things, Lou." Her hand moved under the sheet and came to rest in his.

He thought, wonderingly: has she found someone to bear the anxiety for her at last and does that make the difference?

But why only now? Brade had always been there.

And he thought: have I?

Brade drew a deep breath and began to slip down the shallow decline that led to sleep.

He came down to breakfast the next morning very silent, determined to do nothing to break the fragile web of peace that had existed between himself and Doris. The bacon and eggs were ready, just ready, and Doris smiled briefly and was very quiet, too.

Brade could hear Ginny bustling about in her room. He ate rapidly in order to be gone before her shattering energy burst into the room. He said, gulping down his coffee and blotting his mouth on the napkin, "I might as well go off early, eh?"

"Might as well," said Doris, "and, Lou—"

"Yes?"

"You'll call if—if anything happens?"

"Of course. And if I don't call, you know everything is all right. And—and don't worry." He recalled last night. "I'm in charge."

She smiled tremulously, "All right."

He kissed her with a hard pressure and broke off as he

heard Ginny's shoes clattering down the stairs, "Good-bye."

The students seemed more normal at this lecture. The pull toward the rostrum had weakened and those with a natural tendency to seek the stratospheric reaches of the rear seats were part way there already.

Brade lectured a little more loudly than usual, showing them there was nothing wrong. His formulas were larger as he wrote them on the board, and he went through the addition products of the carbonyl group with an absent facility.

Sulfite addition products and cyanohydrins. Hydrazones, phenylhydrazones, and semicarbazones. He paid his usual special attention to the phenylhydrazones in order to lead into the osazone derivatives of the monosaccharides. He was sharply conscious of the fact that organic chemistry was increasingly the handmaiden of biochemistry and this was one of the numerous places of contact.

So he talked reaction mechanisms for a steady five minutes.

He remained behind after the lecture to answer a few questions—in another return to normality. But then that was done, too, and he picked up his mail in the boxes outside the department office door and began a slow climb to the fourth floor and a return to a world in which a murder had taken place. (Was it to postpone the return that he deliberately chose not to take the elevator?)

He looked through his mail as he climbed. He had not picked it up during the excitement of Friday morning, or, for that matter, on Sunday either, and now he had a three-day accumulation. None of it seemed of importance, however; chemical supply houses peddling their wares in third-class envelopes and book publishers doing the same for theirs.

He paused at a yellow envelope of the type used to hold interdepartmental mail. His own name was typed on it and the return address was a simple: Department of Chemistry. What official communication was he receiving? This was fast work after Saturday's blow-off. He had visions of Littleby bustling in to work this morning with one particular job that needed doing at once.

He stuffed the rest of the mail into his jacket pocket and tore open the yellow envelope. It contained a memo sheet with only a line in it. "The safety course will be listed in the catalog as being given by the department." And it was signed by Littleby.

Brade felt a twitch of surprise. The old man had given in to Brade's hasty growl of Saturday evening. There was no mention, of course, of "bettering his position in the department," but Brade had certainly not expected even this much.

He reached the fourth floor and lifted his head just in time to come face to face with Otto Ranke, coming down from his own offices on fifth floor.

Brade felt the surge of adrenalin in the blood. His upper lip actually lifted in a kind of snarl.

It was Ranke who spoke. With an amazing heartiness, he said, "Lou, old boy, how are you? Look fine, yes, sir."

He clapped the organic chemist on the shoulder with a fast double knock, showed his dentures, and was down the stairs.

Brade stared after him in surprise. Was it as easy as this? Did one bite once to establish the fact that fangs existed and, thereafter, was a snarl alone sufficient? Did it take once to cow Ranke? He looked at the memo sheet he still held in his hand. And Littleby, too?

He found himself at his own office, still dazed, and felt his key turn and catch. The door was already unlocked.

Oh, God, that meant Cap Anson would be there and somehow Brade was in no mood to fiddle with the eternal book. He needed time, instead to think and—

He flung the door open peevishly and stopped at the threshold. Cap Anson was there, yes—but a stranger was there, too.

Cap Anson, cane hooked over his left arm, was at Brade's glass-lined cabinets, taking down the typing-paper boxes which contained the reprints of Brade's papers, together with the original manuscripts and other pertinent details. Each box had the name of the paper on it in neat India-ink lettering, in a style Brade had taken over from Anson himself, as he had taken over so many little professional habits. On the shelf below were the duplicate sheets of the research notebooks of Brade's various students, carefully bound and labelled.

It all looks like the product of a very neat and very dull housewife, Brade throught.

Anson said, "I'm boasting a bit about your work, Brade."

But Brade was looking at the other. He saw a tanned face that looked sixtyish, iron-gray hair, a pronounced stoop and a wide, humorous mouth. He recognized him, of course, with the second glance. He had heard him delivering papers at the A.C.S. conventions. For that matter, he had seen his picture often enough, once on the cover of *Chemical and Engineering News*.

He did not wait for a formal introduction, but put out his hand and said, "Dr. Kinsky."

"Yes. Hello, hello. Dr. Brade, I presume. I've heard of your work." Tight little lines appeared about his mouth and eyes and he nodded his head in little jerks in time to his own phrases. "Followed it with some interest. Fellow students of good old Cap, eh?"

Brade nodded also and wondered if Joseph Kinsky really spared the time to follow the minor work of a minor chemist. He said, "Thank you." He would have gone on to say something about his own knowledge of Kinsky's much more important work but the other hurried on:

"There've been changes since my day, though. Hope you don't mind my making free of your lab. Cap brought me in; the floor is still all his, you know. Goes everywhere. As in my day. No student is safe from him." He looked about with a visible nostalgia. "I used to visit the old school occasionally, but now I haven't been here for fifteen years."

Brade said, "Well, let's all sit down. Are you free for lunch, Dr. Kinsky?"

"Eh? No. No. Afraid not. But thanks anyway. I can't stay long this time, but didn't want to leave without taking a quick look anyway at the old pile. Happy years spent here. Seem happy anyway now that they're over, eh?"

Brade nodded. "I know what you mean. Well, I'm sorry we can't make a day of it. Have you been in town long?"

"Over a week. Should have been here sooner. Personal matters, though. Family. Bound and determined, though, to save the last couple of days for old Cap."

Old Cap! Brade felt irritated at the phrase. Cap was

old, yes; over seventy. But Kinsky was obviously pushing sixty.

But there was Cap, not irritated at all, but gazing at Kinsky fondly, like a husband at his new bride or a mother at her gifted younger child.

Cap was looking at Kinsky, the gifted pupil, the light of chemistry, the honor of his teacher.

And Brade recognized his own feelings as jealousy; he was the neglected, unremarkable student stifling in the glow of the successful one come home.

He forced himself to say, steadily, "I suppose you don't need any comment of mine on your remarkable work in tetracycline synthesis."

"Pooh. Nonsense." Kinsky threw up a hand in humorous deprecation. "No comment worthwhile. Moran-Minter at Cambridge is far ahead of me."

"From a different angle, though. I think you'll get to aldosterone ahead of him."

"That so? That your opinion? Now, it's queer of you to say so. Very queer, considering—"

Cap Anson interrupted. "Young Joe here was kind enough to get away yesterday and spend an evening at my place with the book. He *liked* it." The old man chuckled with satisfied self-approbation.

"Oh, yes. Oh, yes. Chemists need that book. Yes. Too many chemists live in the present only. Mathematicians and physicists know the history of their science because new developments supplement the old. In chemistry, new developments seem to replace the old. Tendency is to forget the old, then; and too much is forgotten in that way. The old is the basis for the new. New can't be understood properly without the old."

"Quite right," murmured Brade.

"And Cap's the fellow to rub that into us, eh? This kind of subject matter needs more than a chemist. Needs a philosopher and that's Cap."

Cap Anson chuckled again and Brade nodded a little hesitantly. A real love feast. He wished this were over. It was depressing him.

Kinsky said, "Of course, in the old days I never thought of old Cap as a philosopher. More as a martinet."

Brade smiled faintly. "He was one in my day, too."

"Oh, he must have toned down. He must have. When I knew him, he was in his thirties. Full of pep and vinegar. Remember, Cap, remember when you wanted me to run the exhaustive methylation of the ring compound and I said it was a waste of time and the dressing-down you gave me. Whew! Talk about nightmares. Skin peeled clean off to my ears. Fact. That was when he got his name. I'll bet you don't even know his real name. I'll bet no one knows without looking it up, eh?" He looked vastly pleased with himself.

Brade was interested. "You mean you're the one who pinned the name Cap on Cap."

"Sure did. Why do you think he's called Cap?"

"I don't really know. I seem to recall there was an old-time ball player named Cap Anson."

"That helped the name catch on, but it had nothing to do with the origins."

"I've heard some people say Cap owned a ship once." Brade saw the possible humor in that. "Maybe a rowboat."

Cap Anson, listening to the exchange with growing wrath, said, "This is nonsense!" He rapped the cane tip against the floor in a peremptory double knock.

"No," said Kinsky, at once. "Not nonsense at all. Authentic bit of Ansoniana. He was flaying me about the exhaustive methylation. The names he called me. Then when I thought he was spiraling down to a roar, he stopped. Looked at me. Hard. He said, 'Kinsky, when you do research for me, just remember I'm captain of the ship. You can think for yourself until such time as I tell you what to think. Then you think my way because I'm captain and you're cabin boy. Understand?' That was it. That was it. I never called him anything but Cap from that day. After a while, no one else called him anything but, either."

Anson glowered. "Nothing of the kind ever happened."

Out of pity for his embarrassed teacher, Brade kicked the matter to one side with an abrupt return to a previous subject. He said, "And if it's something you care to discuss Dr. Kinsky, what are the prospects of a successful aldosterone synthesis?"

"Depends. Depends," said the other, fussily. "My opinion is they're pretty good. But, of course, not yours."

"Not *mine?* Why, I know nothing about it or almost nothing."

"Your student's is what I mean. Oh," and his face took on an automatically lugubrious cast. "Dreadful sorry to hear about the accident."

"Can't be helped," muttered Brade. "Which of my students has been concerned with aldosterone synthesis?"

Kinsky said, with surprise, "The one who died. What's his name—Neufeld. He was perfectly certain my method of attack will never yield aldosterone. Very dogmatic young man. Told me to my face."

"What?" said Brade, explosively. "Have you talked to him?"

"Of course. It was at the A.C.S. meetings in Atlantic City last year."

"I remember he attended. I obtained department funds for him to cover travel expenses. He never mentioned having talked to you."

Kinsky sniffed. "Doubtless considered the matter too unimportant to mention. Came up to me after I gave my paper on the subject, introduced himself, and said flatly I couldn't possibly make my projected synthesis succeed by my methods. Wouldn't tell me what he thought was wrong. Called me a jackass to my face, just about. Whole year now and I haven't forgotten it. Incidentally, Brade, what's going to happen to his problem now that he's dead?"

Was it Brade's hypersensitive imagination or was there really a hard gleam of interest in Kinsky's eyes as he asked the question?

18

BRADE sat there, surprised and thoughtful, looking first at Kinsky and then at Anson, whose pale dry lips had thinned under pressure as though with offense at the memory of their last meeting when that precise subject had arisen.

Brade thought: Well, what do I say?

He tried evasion. "There's been no time to think of the matter properly, Dr. Kinsky."

But Anson broke in peevishly. "He's thinking of continuing it. Against my advice, I might add. I grow old, Kinsky. In the old days, my boys took my advice."

"Well," said Kinsky, uncomfortably, "we all get old."

But a silence fell and the discomfort of the exchange blanketed all three.

Kinsky rose finally and said, "It was a pleasure meeting you, Brade. If you come up my way any time, please feel free to drop in."

"Thank you, I will." Brade shook hands.

Anson said, with traces of sharpness still, "And Brade, I'll be up at five o'clock today to talk over those safety lectures with you. Five o'clock sharp."

"Five o'clock," echoed Brade. It was characteristic of Cap to show no concern over the possibility that Brade might be otherwise engaged at five.

Kinsky said, "And when Cap says five, he doesn't mean five-oh-one. Or has he changed?"

"He hasn't changed," said Brade.

It was a strange bitterness that Brade felt now; the loss of a father whose existence he had not fully realized. But was not Cap Anson a kind of father?

He realized it now. Now that he had seen him standing there with his older son, his successful son, his *good* son, the one who brought back pride and honor, who had done as he was told and had stood still to be excoriated by the captain of the ship.

While Brade—the worthless one, frozen immovably in a job and losing that at last. Being urged on in a new direction by poor Cap and sullenly refusing.

Poor Cap! Grown old with honors and renown and ending insecure anyway. Cap and his book.

Brade thought: Doris is coming back to me, but everything else is going. My graduate students are dying. My research collapses in fakery. My job is gone. And Cap Anson—

He thought in bitter self-mockery: and my father doesn't love me.

He rose to his feet and walked through the connecting back in Anson's early time, but Anson had walled it off door to his laboratory. It had once been part of the office, and had it equipped with vacuum lines, hot and cold running water, steam vents and gas lines.

It had always been Anson's thesis that every professor, however old and however rusty in his joints should never allow himself to forget the feel of a test tube or a pair of forceps. There must always be some experiments, however picayune, however unimportant, that he conducted himself.

Brade followed Anson in this respect, too. Brade's own acid-catalyzed rearrangements under oxygen atmosphere were a minor affair, but that didn't matter. As Anson said, there was a pleasure in doing something with our own hands.

But Brade looked mournfully now at his somewhat rickety set-up and wondered where he might find that pleasure now. At the moment, the gunked-up reaction vessel was only unpleasant. Unpleasant in its hardened contents, unpleasant in the memories to which it gave rise.

He had not touched it since Thursday afternoon, when he had wandered into Ralph's laboratory in search of standard acid and found a dead body. The set-up had been in suspended animation since then from the reaction flask through the glass and plastic tubing to the large, faded-green, compressed-oxygen cylinder.

Automatically, he looked at the cylinder. Funny!

Was the cylinder empty? He had changed it, surely, not long before that last experiment. The inner gauge, the one leading to the body of the five-foot cylinder, should read at least 1800 pounds per square inch, but it didn't. It read zero.

Now why was that?

Had he left it open and had the gas bled away? The outer gauge, the one connected to the outer world, read zero, too. He tested its stopcock and it was closed off. There was no leak.

Well, then, had he shut off the main valve, emptied the gauges of their small oxygen content, and then locked the secondary valve, too? It would have been the neat and proper thing to do, but he didn't remember doing it.

He put his hand on the main valve that topped the cylinder and put clockwise pressure on it. It didn't budge. Obviously it was already closed.

Automatically, his hand exerted counterclockwise pressure to force oxygen into the gauge and watch the needles move—and he paused.

Undoubtedly, his life hung in balance that second and by pausing, he saved it.

It was not his conscious eye that saw it, but his chemist's eye; the inner vision that through twenty-five years of custom saw that which did not fit and paused at it.

That-which-did-not-fit showed up to his conscious eye as a small glisten, as an edge of oily liquid at the rim of the bit of thread that remained between the main gauge and the cylinder itself. He put his fingernail upon it, scraping and then smelling.

He seemed to be alone in a vast silence as he reached for the wrench and fitted the appropriate end upon the hexagonal joint. He exerted force and the valve unwound with a curious slipping that should not have been there.

The gauge came off and all the thread was wet. The needle valve was wet. He could not identify the liquid certainly but it had the thick consistency of glycerol.

If he had actually turned the main valve counterclockwise, the laboratory wall would probably have been blown out with the force of the explosion.

Brade let the gauge clatter down on a laboratory benchtop and sat down with a jar. He was trembling violently with the closeness of death.

When the trembling had subsided (he didn't know how much time had elasped), he rose and made certain the outer door of his laboratory was locked. He then locked his office door. Let them assume he was out for lunch. (Lunch? He felt revolted.)

He found himself staring at the gauges, at the glistening wet and deadly threads.

He had used the cylinder Thursday, the day Ralph had died. It had been in order then, obviously. He had not used the cylinder since and anyone might have been in his office and laboratory since. He was not Ralph. He might lock his office at five, when leaving—if he thought of it. He certainly did not lock when going to the student laboratory, to the library, or even out to lunch.

Of course, Cap Anson had been in his lab twice since Thursday (he had a momentary vision of Cap killing the naughty student who had rebelled against him and it all but forced a wan smile out of him) and Kinsky had been with him the second time. Roberta had been in Ralph's lab, could have been in his own, too. Hell! *anyone* could have been in his lab.

Unwillingly, he thought again of Kinsky. The man *had* been in his lab. Cap Anson had been with him, but Cap was notoriously capable of growing interested in something Kinsky might point out in a book, and of knowing nothing of the world about him for a space of time. Kinsky would know that characteristic. Certainly he would know that.

Without even trying, Brade found himself sketching in the details of the structure. Kinsky had met Ralph. Ralph had boasted that his work would prove Kinsky a jackass. Was Kinsky sufficiently brain-proud to fight that by any deed at all, even by killing Ralph? Would he then plan to kill Brade to avoid having the pupil's work continued by the teacher? He had asked so eagerly if Brade planned to continue the work—and the cylinder was already smeared. Would he have wiped the glycerol away if Brade had convinced him he planned to drop the research? Or were matters past correction and was Kinsky merely indulging a morbid curiosity?

Impossible! It was all impossible! Kinsky had been in town the day of Ralph's death, but how could he know the details of Ralph's experimental ways well enough to plan the details of the murder?

Brade put his cold hands to a flushed forehead. No, it was his jealousy of Kinsky that was pushing these thoughts at him, not his reason.

How could a chemist, unless he were absolutely psychotic, dream of fighting the truth by assassination when another would rediscover—

But anyone might be psychotic.

And what if this had no connection with Ralph's death? (Two murderers at once? Impossible coincidence?) ·But *could* someone have had an independent grudge against Brade himself? Only Saturday night, after all, he had offended Foster bitterly—and Ranke. To the point of murder?

He recalled Ranke's incongruous friendliness on the stairs that morning with a new chill. Was it only the patronizing friendliness of a murderer for a victim as good as dead and no longer worth the expenditure of adrenalin?

Or Littleby? Brade had flicked Littleby's nose, too, and the quick memo of this morning might be just that sort of patronizing sop, too.

Littleby? God! Brade was spinning wildly, gyrating. He was seeing ghosts under the bed if he thought Littleby capable of this sort of thing. Stop it!

At any rate, Doheny must know of this for, in any case, whoever the culprit, it could not be Assistant Professor Louis Brade in this case and, if there were only one murderer, that meant he was innocent in Ralph's case as well.

Almost coldly, he reached for the telephone. He dialed a number and a matter-of-fact voice said, "Police Precinct Nine. Officer Martinelli speaking."

Brade said in a carefully flattened voice. "May I speak to a plainclothesman named Jack Doheny. When do you expect him? I see. No, no," (quickly) "no one else will do. It's not an emergency. Listen, when he checks in or comes in will you tell him I called. I am Professor Louis Brade. He knows me. Tell him I've got to see him as soon as possible My number is University 2-1000, Extension 125. Yes. Yes. Thank you."

He hung up and stared at the phone a long time.

He thought: I'd better eat.

He did not go out to eat but brought a sandwich back to his office, walking quickly and avoiding people. He felt distinctly reluctant to venture out into the world while he did not know who his would-be murderer was. Here, behind locked doors—

Yet here, behind locked doors, death had waited for him.

He drank coffee directly out of the container while it was still too hot and only afterward noticed that he had not added cream.

Then it was closing in on one o'clock and he thought: I'll go down to the laboratory.

He locked the door behind him, feeling the knob over and over again, checking (would he ever be able to leave his office door unlocked again? ever?) and walked the length of the corridor to the student lab.

Charlie Emmett was preparing for the demonstration of semicarbazone formation under pressure. It would mean that in fifteen minutes or so, Emmett would be forming a glass "bomb," closing off the thick walls by slow turning in a flame, producing a seal without thinning, strain or weakness; one which would withstand the several atmospheres of pressure of the heated vapors within once the reaction mixture within the bomb was heated.

Brade always worried about such demonstrations. The possibility of accident always existed, and yet the students had to be shown.

Of course, Emmett was good at this. Brade had seen

him make a bomb tube before. He had watched steady
eyes on steady flame and steady hands turning the con-
stricting end of the tube into a yellow heat.

It needed steady hands and an icy heart to put glycerol
on the threads of an oxygen gauge.

Brade was ashamed of the thought. Charlie Emmett?
Colorless Charlie Emmett? What motive? God help us all,
what motive? (Roberta Goodhue came in, smiled at him
briefly and shakenly, then hurried to the side bench for
some last-minute manipulation of the chemical supply
prepared that morning for the day's experiments.)

Brade looked at his watch. It was five minutes to one.
In five minutes precisely, the students would spill inward.

He mused sadly on the manner in which the teacher's
life was tied to the clock in half a dozen installments of
lectures, lab sessions, seminars and faculty meetings.

Minute hand touched twelve, and a student walked in,
unfolding his black rubber apron as he entered and slipping the loop over his head. He said, dutifully, "Hello,
Professor Brade," put his books down at one of the desks
and opened an acid-burnt laboratory manual.

As he did so, a folded set of papers fell out of the
book, and the student stared at them, first with wonder
and then with consternation. He walked quickly to where
Emmett stood at one end of the lab.

He said, "Say, Mr. Emmett, I guess I forgot to turn in
the report on my first unknown Friday. All right if I hand
it in now?" He looked anxious.

Emmett said with gruff authority, conscious of Brade's
eyes on him, perhaps. "Okay, I'll look at it later. But
watch that sort of thing next time."

Absently, Brade watched the papers handed over to
Emmett. Other students were walking in rapidly now.

Time had spoken. Time, that chops the teacher's day into fragments and pins him to the clock in a kind of temporal crucifixion.

Time—and what had just happened. Good Lord, he thought—

It was as though the students had disappeared and the laboratory with them, and he was alone in the universe with a thought, a twisted, awful thought.

He left the laboratory abruptly. Two or three pairs of eyes turned to look curiously at him, but he was past caring.

He was at the telephone again and he had to look the number up in a book.

"But I must," he explained to the efficient young voice that answered. "It's quite important and will only take a minute or so. No, I can't really wait for 3 P.M."

And he couldn't. He had to know now. This minute.

The wait was unbearable and he cowered inside at the thought of the embarrassment and fright this would mean.

The thin little voice in his ear now *was* frightened and called upon him to identify himself in breathless little gasps.

"Are you sure?" Brade said, finally. "Are you sure? Is that exactly what happened? Exactly?"

He suggested alternates, over and over, until he stopped out of the sheer fear of inducing hysteria.

He asked only once more, "Are you sure?" and then broke connections.

So he knew. He had the motive, the sequence of events, everything.

Or at least he *thought* he knew.

Except that he wasn't an experienced policeman. How

does one go about *proving* a suspicion? For that matter, how does one go about proving a certainty?

He sat quietly thinking until the sun had declined enough to be shining directly into his eyes so that he had to rise to lower the blind. It was then that there was a discreet knock at the door.

This time he recognized the portly figure bulking its outlines through the frosted panel of the door and he opened it hastily. "Come in, Mr. Doheny." Carefully, he locked the door again.

Doheny said, "Afternoon, Professor. Got the call kinda late and thought I'd come right over. Sorry I wasn't on the spot."

"It's all right."

"I ain't interfering with your classes, I hope."

"No."

"Okay, Prof. What's on your mind? I figure a guy like you got to have a lot on his mind to call the police like that."

"I'm afraid so." He watched the stocky detective seat himself and was confronted by his presence. He said, hastily, "Look, there's been an attempt on my life."

And Doheny, who had been reaching into a vest pocket for a cigar, froze, and the friendliness in his eyes was suddenly gone. They grew cold, and he said, "That so? Did you get hurt?"

"No. I escaped. But just one more moment would have finished me."

"A nick of time kind of thing?"

"That's right."

But a cold feeling settled in Brade's stomach. There was no questioning the fact that the detective was staring at him with hostility. No, more than that; for the first time, Doheny looked at Brade as though he had finally brought himself to consider the professor as a probable murderer.

19

BRADE faltered, but slowly described the manner in which he had discovered his oxygen to have been tampered with.

Doheny listened with eyelids half lowered. Only once did he blaze into interest and that was when Brade described the liquid as "glycerol or, as it is more commonly, but incorrectly, called, glycerine."

Doheny said at once, with a tensing of his hands against the edge of the table, "Glycerine? You mean like nitroglycerine?"

Brade suppressed annoyance. "No, no. Glycerine itself—glycerol, I mean—is quite harmless. It's used in candies and cosmetics."

"Harmless? Well then—"

"Harmless under ordinary conditions. But you see, if that cylinder were turned on, pure oxygen would fill the small chamber inside the gauge at a pressure of about 1800 pounds per square inch. As comparison, the pressure of oxygen in the air about us is about 3 pounds per square inch. Under the influence of the high-pressure oxygen, the glycerol, ordinarily harmless, would react rapidly and violently, liberating a quantity of heat—"

"You mean it would explode."

"Yes. That would knock the main valve off the cylinder so that the rest of the oxygen would come rushing out, converting the cylinder itself into a kind of jet-propelled monster. It would have wrecked the laboratory and would certainly have killed me."

Doheny drew in a deep breath and scratched one plump cheek with a rigid fingernail. He said, "Could the stuff've got on by accident?"

"No," said Brade, firmly. "The threads on an oxygen cylinder must never be lubricated and certainly I can't imagine anyone doing so just by accident. The tank was in perfect order last Thursday, and what has happened is that it has been tampered with deliberately."

"To kill you, Prof. That right?"

"Obviously. There can be no other reason. I use the tank and no one else does. It was only a matter of time before I turned the main valve. I was within a hair's breadth of doing it, in fact."

Doheny nodded. There was no easing of the coldness in his manner. "And what do you figure this means? Figure the same guy poisoned your boy and smeared that oxygen thing?"

Brade said, "Two separate killers in this place would be stretching coincidence, wouldn't it?"

"Sure would. And so you figure the killer ain't you, anyway, cause you're one of the victims?"

"Well—"

"But actually, you ain't one of the victims, are you, Prof? You're safe as if you were sitting in church cause you never turned the valve. Sure you didn't put the goo on yourself, Professor?"

"What! Look here—"

"No. *You* lookit. This makes me feel lousy. It makes me feel like maybe I've been wrong. I had you figured as not guilty, against the evidence. Now you've got guilt rubbed off on yourself cause you couldn't sit still."

An animation entered Dohney's words as he went on. "A guy under suspicion could, if he's guilty, sit around and do nothing and figure the police won't come up with jury evidence. That's maybe the best thing to do, also the hardest. *You* can't do it on account of you got imagination; you're the type who sits around thinking up things to get nervous over.

"Next best thing is to take it on the lam, make tracks. *You* can't. You got a family; you got a position. So that leaves the other thing a guilty man can do. He can counterattack. He can manufacture evidence to clear him. To do that kind of thing, the suspect's gotta figure he's smarter than the police. That's an easy thing for a professor to figure. I mean, smartness is his trade, see?"

Brade interrupted energetically, "I tell you none of this is so in my case."

"All right, Prof, I hear you. But let's follow it up. The most usual kind of fake evidence we come across is the kind where the suspect fixes it to look like he's another victim. I mean if there's houses being burgled somewhere and we figure the burglar is one of the guys in the neighborhood, it ain't unusual to find that our suspect's house gets itself burgled. Then he's just one of the victims. *He* can't be the burglar, can he?"

"And so I tampered with the cylinder myself and called you."

"Professor, I like you. But I think that's just what you did."

Brade picked up the gauge and said, calmly, "You don't want this for evidence, then?"

"It ain't evidence for anything."

Brade nodded. He wiped the threads on the gauge and on the cylinder with a soft rag dipped first in alcohol and then in ether. He blew compressed air over them. "I'll go over this more carefully later." He tightened the gauge back onto the cylinder with an angry twist of the wrench.

He put the wrench down and turned on Doheny, who had been watching him attentively.

Brade said, "You're using a psychology which I see through, Mr. Doheny. You're trying to make it seem that you're weaving a web of logic about me and think that I will therefore break down into a confession through desperation, and that then you'll have your precious jury evidence. It won't work."

"Why not?"

"Because it would only work on a guilty man and I'm not guilty. As a matter of fact, I know who is."

Doheny smiled broadly. "Using psychology on *me*, Professor?"

"I wouldn't know how."

"All right. Who's the killer?"

Brade felt goaded to desperation by the other's patient air of humoring an eccentric. He said, "I need the jury evidence, too, and I'll get it for you. Just watch me."

He looked quickly at his watch, moved to his telephone, and dialed an extension number. "Oh, it's you. Good, this is Professor Brade. The second lab section is about done, isn't it? All right, would you come to my office right now, please? Yes."

He hung up. "Just a few seconds now, Mr. Doheny."

Roberta knocked on the door lightly and Brade let her in. She was wearing a gray laboratory coat, several sizes too large, stained red about the upper pocket where she kept the glass-marking pencils, and discolored and pitted by chemicals.

She brought with her the faint odor of the organic laboratory; an odor students began by disliking and grew to disregard.

Her face seemed unlit, somehow, as though the fires of life behind it were banked low. Her eyes flickered away from focus.

Brade thought, despite himself: poor thing.

He said, "Roberta, this gentleman is Mr. Jack Doheny."

Her eyes drifted momentarily to Doheny. She murmured, "How do you do?"

Brade said, "He's the detective in charge of the case."

The girl's eyelids lifted and life flared. "Ralph's accident?"

"Mr. Doheny thinks the death was not accidental. Nor do I. It was murder."

She was ablaze now. "Why do you say that?" Her eyes shifted on the detective, fixed on him. "I knew he couldn't have made that stupid mistake. Who did it? Who did it?"

Brade thought: she accepts it quickly. She takes to it.

He said, "We're trying to decide that. Meanwhile there's something else. Mr. Doheny has, I'm afraid, found out about your friendship with Ralph."

She looked carelessly contemptuous. "That's no surprise."

"Oh?"

"Mrs. Neufeld—Ralph's mother—said the police were asking." She said to Doheny, "You might have asked me. I would have told you."

Doheny smiled, then said gently, "Didn't like to bother you, miss, unless I had to. This ain't any fun for you, I guess."

"No, it isn't."

Brade said, "Mr. Doheny found out that Ralph and you had quarreled."

She said, "When?"

Brade said, "Sit down, Roberta. Please. There's just something I want to straighten out and I think you can help me do so. Please sit down."

Roberta hesitated, then lowered herself slowly into the seat nearest the door. "What's this about quarreling, Professor Brade?"

"At a soda fountain."

She looked surprised and so, to a lesser extent, did Doheny.

Brade said, "It was a matter of disagreement as to the nature of the sundae you were going to order."

Roberta shook her head. "I don't recall any such thing at all. Who told you this?" She kept looking from one to the other, harried, wary.

Doheny volunteered nothing. Brade thought: he's giving me rope, playing out loop after loop of it and waiting for me to trip and come up swinging by the neck.

He said, "As I heard it, you ordered a chocolate fudge sundae and there was an argument about it."

"No."

"Or at any rate, the soda clerk heard a whispered argument, and he definitely heard the word 'fudge' and then you ordered a fudge sundae."

He paused and Roberta said nothing, but her eyes seemed to grow large and swim in a whitening face.

Brade said, "Would you explain, for Mr. Doheny's benefit, the fact that the soda clerk might not have understood what he heard. Would you explain a second meaning of the word 'fudge'?"

She said nothing.

Brade said, "A meaning of particular significance to students."

She said nothing.

He said, "Roberta, am I wrong in suggesting that to fudge data is to fake them? Was your argument about fudged data rather than about fudge sundaes?"

"No," she began, breathlessly.

"Yesterday, I found you in Ralph's laboratory going through his notebooks. Were you looking for keepsakes, Roberta? Or were you looking for the faked data? Perhaps you wanted to destroy them for the sake of Ralph's reputation?"

Roberta managed to shake her head.

Brade said, "No use denying it, Roberta. I went through the books, too. And *I* found the fudged figures."

"It wasn't so," she cried out, violently. "I mean, you don't understand. It wasn't the way you make it sound. He was desperate. Ralph didn't know what he was doing."

Brade frowned. "Good heavens, Roberta, of course he knew what he was doing. His dishonesty was spread out over months. Don't defend him. There is no defense for a thing like that."

"I tell you, he wasn't thinking straight. He had to get his degree. That was all he knew. He was so sure of his theory that he thought it was just a matter of time till he got the proper data and—"

"And meanwhile he fudged some data to have it to fall back upon in case the proper data didn't show up? Is that it?"

"I swear, Professor Brade, he wasn't going to use those figures, ever. I mean—" She put out her hands helplessly, gesturing the words that would not come. She managed to swallow and said, "He would have told you. He would have come to you before ever coming up for his orals."

"Did he tell you he would?" said Brade. Pity for her kept welling up and would not be damned back.

"I *know* he would have."

Doheny interrupted finally, leaning forward on the desk. "Professor, if you don't mind, I'll just interrupt a minute. Miss, could you tell me one thing? How'd you get to know about this fudging deal? Your boy friend didn't just go ahead and tell you, did he?"

"No. No." For a moment, she stared blankly at the detective. Then she said, "I have a key to his lab. Sometimes I came in when he wasn't expecting me. One time, I tiptoed up behind him, you know—"

Doheny nodded. "Gonna put your hands over his eyes or tickle him or something. Sure. I know. Go on."

"He was busy with his notebook. I saw what he was doing. He was getting figures out of thin air to fit an equation. I said, 'What are you doing?' "

She closed her eyes, remembering.

Doheny said, "And he told you?"

She shook her head. "No. He—he hit me. It was the only time, ever. He jumped out of his chair and hit out at me and just stared at me like a wild man. Then he was sorry and took—took me in his arms, but—"

"But you knew what he had been doing?"

"Yes."

"When was all this?"

"About three weeks ago, I think."

"And that's what you were arguing about at the soda fountain? You were trying to get him to quit and start over?"

"Yes."

Doheny sat back again and raised his eyebrows at Brade. He said, "You win this round, Prof. You're no dummy." He looked a little cheered. "Got anything more up your sleeve?"

"I'm not sure," began Brade and the door to his office opened.

Brade looked up.

Cap Anson, key in one hand, cane in the other, stood in the doorway.

The old man stared in open displeasure at the others present and without any acknowledgement or greetings said, "We had an appointment, Brade."

"Oh, Good Lord, yes," said Brade, with instant contrition, looking at his watch. It was five, precisely. "Look, Cap, give me ten minutes, will you? If you'll sit down, we'll be through here soon."

He got up, walked around Anson and closed the door, then placed a gentle hand on the old man's shoulder, and forced him into a seat. "It won't take long."

Cap Anson looked meaningfully at his watch. "We have a lot of work to do."

Brade nodded and turned back to Roberta. "The point is this, now, Roberta. How did all this affect your relations with Ralph? I mean, all this about fudged results?"

Anson leaned forward, spoke before anyone else could. "What's this about fudged results?"

Brade said, "Ralph apparently made up his experimental results to fit his theories. This, by the way, is Plainclothesman Doheny, the officer in charge of the case. This is Professor Anson."

Anson did not acknowledge the introduction. He said, violently, "Then what was all that last Saturday about continuing that boy's work?"

"I only found out on Sunday, yesterday,"' said Brade. "But Roberta, you still haven't told me. How were your relations with Ralph affected?"

"Well, we argued, but that's all. I understood what was driving him. I knew he wouldn't—he would straighten it out."

"Did *he* say so?"

Roberta was silent.

Brade said, "Look, Roberta. You know how Ralph was. He was very suspicious. He had a tendency to assume other people were against him. Now, didn't he?"

"He'd gone through a great deal."

"I'm not judging him. I'm simply trying to state a fact. You were one of the very few people he accepted and tried to trust and now you had spied on him and were accusing him and badgering him. You had become one of his persecutors, one of his enemies. Do you see what I'm driving at?"

Doheny interrupted again. "Say, Prof, the way you're going, it looks like you're gonna prove the boy killed the young lady. She ain't dead, you know."

"I realize that," said Brade at once, "but if Ralph began to think of Roberta as an enemy, he might not kill her, but he would certainly withdraw and break off their engagement. He has a record of abandoning girls, and there's nothing at all unlikely that he would decide to abandon this one."

Roberta shook her head. "No."

Brade continued, brutally, "And there is nothing at all unlikely in a girl, being cast out, taking her revenge in her own way."

Roberta cried, "What are you saying?"

"That you might have killed Ralph."

"But that's crazy."

"Do you suppose someone else might have killed him over the fudged data?" said Brade, coldly. "Who else would know? Did anyone ever hear you two arguing about it?" He had risen to his feet, leaning toward the girl.

She shrank back, "No—I mean, I don't know."

"Did you ever quarrel with him about the matter, loudly, late at night, in his lab."

"Y-yes. Once."

"And who overheard you? Who was walking through the halls and overheard you?"

"No one. I don't know. No one."

Cap Anson interrupted and said, "See here, Brade, why are you browbeating the poor girl?"

Brade shook him off. He said, "Who overheard you, Roberta?"

"I tell you, no one. How can I know?"

"Was it he?" And Brade's finger stabbed violently in the direction of Cap Anson.

20

CAP Anson said, angrily, "What is this?" and for a moment, the tableau held; Brade and his pointing finger; Anson indignant, his cane half lifted; Roberta is gathering tears, and Doheny, watching it all without expression.

Brade had to lower his arm. He was appalled. He had improvised matters so carefully. He knew Anson would be in at precisely five and he had led Roberta to the proper point at that moment, then dragged her helter-skelter into the abyss so that at the point of maximum intensity, he might shift the full weight of guilt from her to Anson.

What had he expected? That Anson would break down, babble out a confession? That he would have his jury evidence?

He had. He was forced to admit it; he had expected just that.

Doheny said, "Like the man says, Professor, what is this?"

Heavy-hearted, Brade said, "Cap did it."

"Did what?" demanded Anson.

"Killed Ralph. You killed Ralph, Cap."

"This is slander," said Anson, angrily.

"This is truth," said Brade, depressed. How did one go about making a thing like this stick? "You overheard Ralph and Roberta quarreling. Who else wanders the corridors at night? It's a life-long habit with you. You found out that Ralph was using invented results."

"Your saying so doesn't make it so, Brade. But even if I had found out, what follows?"

"It follows that he was my student, Cap, and I was yours." Brade rose, faced the older man tensely. For the moment, only the two of them, eyes locked, mattered. "Ralph's actions reflected on me, Cap, but a reflection on me reflected in turn upon you. Your professional honor was at stake."

"My professional honor," said Anson, voice trembling, "is safe. Nothing can hurt it."

"I think differently. I think that all your life you have held on to it with both hands—desperately. You remember what Kinsky said about you this morning, Cap. You called yourself captain of the ship of research. You were captain, your students the crew. And the captain of a ship on the high seas has the power of life and death over his crew, hasn't he—captain?"

"I don't know what you mean."

"I mean you've always wanted the power of life and death over your students, if not consciously, then unconsciously—or you wouldn't have cherished being called Cap. And now you found that your student; the student of your student, and therefore still *your* student; had committed the worst sin in the scientific decalog; the one unforgiveable sin; the one mortal sin. And you condemned him to death. You had to. If you had let him live and the truth had come out, your reputation—"

Doheny interrupted, his voice unexpected and therefore

startling. "You mean, Prof, the old fellow sneaked into the boy's lab and bollixed the little flasks."

"He had a master key," said Brade.

"And how'd he know what the student was doing? Did he sneak in regular and look over his notes?"

"He didn't have to. He was always in *my* lab. He was here Friday, for instance, when I walked in after lecture. He was here this morning after lecture. For that matter, he just walked in half an hour ago. And the duplicates of Ralph's work, fake figures and all, are here in my office. In his notes, Ralph described his experiments carefully, down to his method of preparing flasks in advance. Cap would have known just what to do and he did it. His own meticulousness made it easy for him to understand and use Ralph's."

"These are all unsupported statements," said Anson. "I don't have to answer them."

Brade said, desperately, "Then when he found I was going to continue Ralph's work—" He paused for breath, and brought out his handkerchief to wipe his forehead. "You tried to pull me off Ralph's work, Cap. You tried at the zoo, Saturday; you tried to interest me in comparative biochemistry. When you failed you condemned me to death, too. I was going to disgrace you so you decided—"

Doheny rose with a look of concern spreading over his wide face. "Professor," he expostulated, "take it easy. One thing at a time. Stick to the boy. Stick to the boy."

Brade passed his handkerchief over his face again. "All right," he said, "I'll stick to the boy, and I'll bring up the one point that proves it. It proved it. That man," his finger shook as he pointed to Cap again, "is the slave of time. All teachers must be, but he's much more so than most. He keeps his appointments to the minute. He came in here today at five on the minute."

"I noticed that," said Doheny.

"All the rest of us humor him. We keep appointments with him to the minute and he's come to expect it. He makes no allowance for lateness. But last Thursday, when I had a five o'clock appointment with him, I *couldn't* keep it because Ralph was dead in his laboratory and I had to stay at school. How did you know that, Cap? How did you know in advance that on that one day of all days I wouldn't be there to keep my appointment when always before I'd been so careful to be on time? When had I ever missed an appointment before that? What possible right did you have to expect me to miss that one?"

"What are you talking about?" said Anson, contemptuously.

"Thursday afternoon," said Brade, "at the stroke of five, you met my little girl in the street on the way to keep an appointment with me. You hadn't been at school that day. No one had informed you of Ralph's death. Yet you gave Ginny a portion of the manuscript of your book. You said, 'Gives this to your father when he comes home.' What made you think I wasn't home?"

"Well, you weren't," said Anson. "Do you deny that?"

"Of course, I wasn't, but how did you know? You didn't ask Ginny if I were home? You didn't come to the door. You just handed over the manuscript and said, 'Give this to your father when he comes home.' '*When* he comes home.' You knew I wasn't home, this one time of all times. You knew I was at school sitting with death. How could you know that, Cap? *How could you know that, Cap?*"

Anson said, "Please don't shout."

"You had arranged the appointment with death. You knew Ralph was dead because you had poisoned the Thursday Erlenmeyer flask. You knew I was bound to discover the body when I stopped in to say goodnight, and that I would be sure to do that because saying goodnight to one's research students was one of the habits I had picked up from you. Only, even so, you couldn't break your habit of keeping appointments and you came to my house to deliver the manuscript."

Anson said, "This is all very foolish. Your daughter said you weren't home."

"You never asked her."

"I did."

"No, Cap. She told me originally that you had said to give me the manuscript when I came home. When I recalled this earlier today, I thought that might not be the whole story. So I called her at school. I made her repeat. I questioned her over and over. You did not ask her if I were home. You assumed it. You knew it."

Anson looked at Doheny. "Surely my word would hold against that of a child. She doesn't remember. I don't see that she can. It was a casual exchange of words that took place four days ago."

Doheny said, "Professor Brade, it's like the other professor says. A jury won't believe this."

Brade said, "But I've worked it out for you. Motive, opportunity. The sequence of events. It all fits."

"Sure it all fits," agreed Doheny, "but lots of things can fit. I can make up a story that'll fit you as murderer, or the young miss here, or someone else. Ain't that the way it is in chemistry, too? Can't you figure out lots of different theories to account for some experiment or other?"

"Yes," said Brade, blankly.

"You gotta find one you can prove by more experiments. It's all well and good to sit down and work out a line of logic, you know, but you'd be surprised what a defense attorney can do to a line of logic if that's all you got."

Brade bowed his head. He had done his best and it hadn't worked.

Doheny said, "I could take Professor Anson in, question him, but that wouldn't look so good if he was innocent. He's a big man in his line, well thought of. I'd need something better to hold on to than just a bunch of logic. I gotta have something solid to hold on to like this thing here." He pounded the oxygen cylinder with a closed fist so that it thumped hollowly. "Something I can yank on and twist." He seized the main valve—

And Anson, cane raised wildly, leaped to his feet in horror. *"Get away from that, you blithering idiot—"* His cane whistled down.

Doheny moved quickly, catching the cane in mid-air, and drawing Anson close. "Something wrong with this here cylinder, Professor Anson?" he asked softly. "What makes you think that?"

The signs of dissolution came suddenly over Cap Anson's face; a look of oldness beyond age.

"How do you know something's wrong with this?" demanded Doheny once more.

Roberta screamed, "You poisoned him. You poisoned him," and threw herself forward. Brade caught her, pinning her arms.

Anson's head had twisted sharply to face the girl. He said, hoarsely, "He deserved it. He was a traitor to science."

"You poisoned him, then?" said Doheny. "You're in

front of witnesses, Professor. Don't say anything you don't mean."

"I should have taken care of him first." He pointed at Brade and shrieked, *"Incompetent!* I told you the morning after that *you* did it and you had. You were responsible by being such a fool as to let him fake data. You made his death necessary." And from a wild cry, he descended to a whisper and said, "Yes, I poisoned Ralph Neufeld," and huddled down into a chair.

They were alone in Brade's office, Brade and Doheny. Doheny had washed his hands and was rubbing them vigorously now on a paper towel.

Brade said, "Will they be hard on him?" With the fury of the moment spent, Cap was just Cap to him again, an old loved man, a peculiar man but a great chemist and his own teacher, almost his own father. The thought of him in prison, in disgrace—

Doheny said, "My guess is he won't come to trial." He tapped his forehead with a stubby forefinger.

Brade nodded sadly.

Doheny said, "Look, Prof, I just wanta say I'm glad my feeling about you was right to begin with. Sorry I doubted you for a while there."

"It's your job to doubt."

"Right. And you did a damned good detective job yourself for an amateur."

"Did I?" Brade smiled faintly.

"Sure. You worked it out. Maybe if I had the facts you had I coulda done it, too, but, you know, prob'ly not so good and not so fast."

Brade said, thoughtfully, "You know, I must have had it all the time, really, ever since my little girl told me what

Cap had said. But I couldn't get myself to believe Cap had done it, so I just—put the thought away from me. Good Lord, when I found my oxygen cylinder had been tampered with, I thought of Cap first, then laughed. After all, what motive could he have had, I thought? Just that I had refused to abandon Ralph's research. I didn't know then that he knew about the fakery, that he conceived his life's reputation to be at stake. The security of his fame." He bowed his head.

Doheny said, "Just when did you catch wise, anyway?"

"When lab started today," said Brade. "It was a little thing. I was thinking of how bound we teachers are to the clock and that always makes me think of Cap. And as I was thinking that, a student handed papers to the boy in charge of the lab and that made me think of Cap's involvement in a similar incident—when he handed papers to Ginny. All I had to do was think of it and everything fell into place."

Doheny said, "Like I said—a real good job. Only thing is, you almost spoiled it talking too much. Know what I mean?"

"Oh?"

"That's where the amateur part comes in. You was gonna tell the old man the whole business, but why? If he was guilty, he knows the whole business. See? So you *don't* tell him everything. You leave out something. Like with the cylinder. You didn't have to tell him about that. If I hadn't of stopped you, you would've spilled it. Then what?

"As it is, you just tell him part of the story, and since he knows the whole thing, he can't keep it straight in the excitement just what parts you told him and what parts you didn't. Then you maneuver him into telling you the part you *didn't* tell him. Get it? Then he's caught, like when he showed he knew something was wrong with the cylinder."

"Well, thank you for that, Mr. Doheny."

The detective shrugged. "Just a trick of the trade. An old one, but the good ones are all old, gotta be. Well, I guess we say good-bye now, Prof. Hope we don't meet no more. In the way of business, I mean."

Brade shook hands absently, looked about his office as though he had never seen it before. He said, "You know, this whole thing took just under a hundred hours. "That's all."

"Seemed a lot longer, I'll bet."

"A lifetime," said Brade.

Doheny cocked his head to one side and said, "What will this whole thing do to your job?"

"What? Oh, well, you know," there was a trace of wildness in Brade's short laugh, "I don't really care. Once I found out the job was gone, it was like a big clamp letting go of me. Losing meant I didn't have to *worry* about losing. It was relief! Do I make sense?"

"I don't know if it's sense, but I get what you mean, Professor."

"When Cap finally told me my job was lost—" Brade fell into a sudden study. Had Cap been telling him the truth, by the way? Had Littleby really decided not to renew the appointment? Or had it been part of Cap's campaign to twist Brade away from Ralph's work. Had it been a piece of psychological warfare? After all, Littleby's conciliatory memo this very morning—

But who cared? It was with a sharp relief that Brade realized that, after all, he didn't give a damn one way or the other.

"I don't give a damn," he said loudly. "I've spent enough of my life in holding tight and trying to go unnoticed. It's a hell of a lot more fun fighting back. Handing it out to Ranke and Foster showed me what could be done when there was no longer reason to hide and when I could afford to fight. But you don't know about that."

Doheny watched him with the bright interested eye of the amateur student of human relations. He said, "This whole thing was one hell of a good fight on your part, Prof."

Brade said, with sudden energy, "So it was. The whole thing." (Of course it was. He had fought against everything from the possible loss of job and family to the possible gain of an electric chair.) He said, slowly, "And I won out."

"You sure did, Professor."

Brade laughed with relief and enjoyment. He thought of Littleby. The poor slob had his own problems. He had a murderer and a victim in his department. He would have to outface the dean of the Graduate School (a cat-smiled tyrant with a brutal ego) on this matter. And the dean would have to outface the president of the university. And the trustees were beyond that and the newspapers beyond them.

Up and down the line, no one was secure. Each had his own devil to fight.

And the lucky man was the man with the guts to fight.

As Brade had done. As *he*, Brade had done.

Brade said, "I'll go home now. I'll be late again, and Doris ought to know about this."

Doheny said, "Don't worry about the lady. I figured you were too keyed up to think of it, so I called her and said everything was okay. I said you might be a little late, because I thought the boys might call to have you come down and answer a few questions."

"Oh?"

"But it looks like they won't so you go on home. If I do need you, just for information, I know where to get you."

"Surely. And thank you, Mr. Doheny."

They shook hands once again and left the building together. Brade turned away to head down the flight of stairs outside the building toward the parking lot.

He turned back a last time. "And Mr. Doheny, the funny thing is I've got tenure now after all these years. It doesn't matter what happens to my job; I've got tenure in the only place it counts. In here." He tapped his chest.

He clattered down the stairs, scarcely caring whether the detective had understood him.

He was going home to Doris, now—with tenure.

Isaac Asimov

☐ BEFORE THE GOLDEN AGE, Book I	22913-0	1.95
☐ BEFORE THE GOLDEN AGE, Book II	Q2452	1.50
☐ BEFORE THE GOLDEN AGE, Book III	23593-9	1.95
☐ THE BEST OF ISAAC ASIMOV	23653-6	1.95
☐ BUY JUPITER AND OTHER STORIES	23062-7	1.50
☐ THE CAVES OF STEEL	Q2858	1.50
☐ THE CURRENTS OF SPACE	23507-6	1.50
☐ EARTH IS ROOM ENOUGH	23383-9	1.75
☐ THE END OF ETERNITY	23704-4	1.75
☐ THE GODS THEMSELVES	23756-7	1.95
☐ I, ROBOT	Q2829	1.50
☐ THE MARTIAN WAY	23783-4	1.75
☐ THE NAKED SUN	22648-4	1.50
☐ NIGHTFALL AND OTHER STORIES	23188-7	1.75
☐ NINE TOMORROWS	Q2688	1.50
☐ PEBBLE IN THE SKY	23423-1	1.75
☐ THE STARS, LIKE DUST	23595-5	1.75
☐ WHERE DO WE GO FROM HERE?—Ed.	X2849	1.75

Buy them at your local bookstore or use this handy coupon for ordering:

FAWCETT BOOKS GROUP, P.O. Box C730, 524 Myrtle Avenue, Pratt Station
Brooklyn, N.Y. 11205

Please send me the books I have checked above. Orders for less than 5
books must include 60¢ for the first book and 25¢ for each additional book to
cover mailing and handling. Postage is FREE for orders of 5 books or more.
Check or money order only. Please include sales tax.

Name	Books $
Address	Postage
	Sales Tax
City_____ State/Zip_____	Total $

Please allow 4 to 5 weeks for delivery

BESTSELLERS